ETHAN & JAG DESTROY THE WORLD

MAZ MADDOX

D1520584

CONTENTS

To the real Halloween Queen: Jess.
Thanks for being my spooky best friend and all around badass.

PREFACE

You'll notice this story is broken up into two parts: *Demon All the Way* and *Ethan & Jag Destroy the World*.

The first part of this book – *Demon All the Way* -- was actually a short story I released as a holiday freebie a couple of years back. It was a fun little Christmas themed short that brought me a ton of joy to write.

Ethan and Jag were so much damn fun that I knew I was going to have to give him more of a story, so I expanded on their lives together in *Ethan & Jag Destroy the World*.

If you've already read *Demon All the Way*, feel free to jump ahead to part II! This is all new stuff nine months after all the shenanigans from *Demon All the Way*.

Otherwise, if this is all new for you, I hope you enjoy this ridiculous little romp between a grumpy demon warrior and a sweet human linguistic nerd.

- Maz

DEMON ALL THE WAY

ROUGH TRANSLATION

Jagmarith, second son of Bolor'gath, Champion of the Blood Wars, and carrier of his clan's armor, sat with his familiar outside of his keep. It was a hot afternoon, the sun in his realm as brutal as the wasteland he called home, and he kept himself cool in the shade while polishing his sword. There hadn't been a war worth donning his armor in ages, but he kept himself ready to be called to action at any moment.

The monotony of the long days was settling into his bones.

Each day, he trained until his muscles ached, honed his weapons so they remained razor sharp and perfect, and tended to his war beast, with whom he had conquered the battle fields many years ago. Keeping a routine in this way was a practice in discipline.

But it was very, very boring.

"Are you not hungry, Master?" Sami, his familiar, asked as he refilled his goblet. "You normally really love roasted chaos boar."

Jag grunted. "My appetite fails me today." He tilted his sword to peer into the reflection of the black metal blade. In the mirror finish of his scarred sword, Jag could see his tired, molten-orange eyes staring back at him. The flush of his crimson skin was dull from lack of excitement, and the broad, mighty black horns that spiraled from his skull needed a fresh coat of wax. Even the ink-black hair that he kept in a tight bun behind his head looked lazy.

With a sigh, Jag lifted his goblet and swallowed a mouthful of a tart liquid, the bite cutting into his jaw before softening into a sweet nectar. Jag narrowed his eyes at his goblet.

"What is this strange concoction?"

"Lemonade!" Sami beamed, his tiny, sharp teeth bright against his green skin. "It's made from sour fruit and sugar. Do you like it?"

Jag tried it again and nodded. "Yes. Is this another strange food from the human realm?" When Sami nodded, Jag curled his lip. "What is your fascination with such weak creatures?"

"They're weak compared to the might of the demons, Master, but they're still interesting in their own right. Their realm has so many unique things." Sami set the pitcher down so he could speak with his hands, gesturing wildly as he spoke. "Did you know they have ice that rains down from the sky in such quantities that it can bury people alive? Can you imagine?"

That sounded nightmarish. Ice falling from the sky? It made Jag shiver to imagine such a horrible event.

Humans and their realm had always been a source of conflict among the warring clans and their enemies. For centuries, they fought over who owned the right to claim the humans as their own and to take their realm and all the treasures it possessed. After much bloodshed, war, and alliances being built and then falling apart, the Demon Empire called a truce.

And the humans remained free. For now.

Jag had never understood why they were so important anyway. The small beings were fragile, hornless, and soft. They didn't even know about the demons that fought for their realm, oblivious to all things except their vanity, electronics, and coffees. Strange, weird little primates, the lot of them.

"It's winter in the human realm right now," Sami continued

with glee. "This is the time of year it gets cold and the ice falls from the sky. But they also have the best food this time of year, Master. So many spices and combinations of meat and pastries. I can't wait to cook them for you!"

"Visiting the human realm is dangerous. Be mindful. Especially if there's falling ice." Jag pushed to his feet and sheathed his sword with practiced ease. And because Jag couldn't allow Sami to think he was genuinely worried about his well-being, he added, "Summoning another familiar to replace you would be inconvenient."

"Of course, Master." Sami gathered up the goblet and weapon-cleaning supplies. "I'll be careful."

The heat of the day and the redundancy of his daily routine had taken their toll on Jagmarith. He no longer wished to peer out into the wasteland and dream of victories. He longed for something new and thrilling. A battle would be ideal, but even different scenery would suffice. Perhaps he was due for another trip to the broiling tar pits or salt mountains.

But even those sounded dull.

Aggravated with his current surroundings, Jag migrated into his large keep to nap. Slumber might improve his mood if only a bit. It might even help inspire him about what to do with his time.

What does a warrior do if there are no wars to fight?

Maybe he needed a pet. A plated grizzly could be entertaining, or perhaps a feral goblin or a cat. All viable options.

As Jag entered his bedchamber, his exhaustion morphed into a small ripple of dizziness. He paused, blinking quickly, and turned his attention inward. Was he sick? Illness wasn't something that often befell mighty demon warriors such as himself, but it was possible. Had the lemony sugar water thrown him off somehow?

No. Impossible. The mighty Jagmarith couldn't be swayed by some fruit and processed sugars.

He tried to laugh at the thought, but then the dizziness caused the room to tilt viciously. Jag nearly tumbled, catching himself against the doorway as he tried to blink his vision back into focus. His stomach flipped, the room spinning, his eyesight blurring around the edges.

Poison? Had his loyal familiar been corrupted somehow? Was that even *possible*? He had summoned Sami himself nearly a century ago from a couple of drops of blood and a handful of razor bat wings. Sami was bound by that spell to be his companion until the day he died.

Not poison. He refused to believe poison.

"Sami!" Jag swallowed back a wave of nausea, sweat beading across his brow. Something was very wrong. The brutal push of gravity had him falling against his doorway, sliding down as the world around him twisted. A bizarre rush of cold swam over him as he tipped backwards into darkness.

Jag fell into the void, a cold vacuum of blackness that spun him through the air like a falling star before he finally crashed down. Feeling the ground under his feet again surprised him, causing him to stagger forward and grip his sword hilt.

The blackness melted away from his vision as reality came to a slow, uneasy stop.

Jagmarith, second son of Bolor'gath, Champion of the Blood Wars, and carrier of his clan's armor, was standing in a place he did not know.

His bedchamber was gone. Instead of his massive estate with the onyx stone keep he had crafted from the black mountains of his homeland, he was surrounded by cream-colored walls of painted cement. The smells of roasting chaos boar and the dry, arid landscape of the wasteland were replaced with the smells of floral soap and dust. Cardboard boxes, half fallen in, lined one wall. A machine lazily spun linen in a circle.

Jag scanned his surroundings, rotating in a slow circle as he tried to make sense of what he was seeing. His fingers twitched on his hilt, ready to strike. Then he heard the faintest of gasps from behind him. A lifetime of war sent his body into action, his sword sliding free as he spun on his heels toward whatever bastard had come to try and claim his head.

But it was no warrior. No rival clan or sworn enemy ready to face him in a battle to the death.

It was much worse.

It was a *human*.

Jag had never seen one up close, only seen pictures of the little, wormy things in books and paintings. He had stayed far away from their realm, vowing to only go there once his clan had won claim to it in battle.

Humans were so much smaller than he had realized.

The one before him stared with eyes as wide as shields, their coloring an earthy green that he'd never seen before. Its skin was a fair shade of ashen white, the mop of curls on its head the color of sunshine. Clutched in its hands was a tome that seemed familiar, the black cover worn like old leather and stitched together like patches.

Jag curled his lip at the human and pointed the tip of his blade at it.

"Why am I here?"

The human opened its mouth to speak, but fear seemingly crippled its ability to do much beyond flap its mouth.

"I won't ask you again, human." Jag took a step forward. "Why am I here?"

The human shook its head, its voice a squeak. "I-I didn't mean to. It was an accident."

"What was?" Jag eyed the book in its hands before pinning his gaze back on the pale human. When there was no response from the terrified worm, Jag bellowed, "Answer me!"

The human screamed, stumbling backward and tripping over its own feet like a small child. It fell, landing on its backside, sending the book sliding across the floor. Jag scoffed at the human's weakness, dropping his sword as he turned his attention to the fallen book. Something about it caught his eye, the scribbling across the pages something he recognized.

With the tip of his blade, he slid the book closer to himself, stooping to pick it up and examine it. Careful script in his mother tongue was written across coarse paper, the ink dried blood and laced with powerful magic. The cover of the book was a leathery skin, pieces of flesh stitched together.

Jag knew of these books. Written by a human piloted by one of his own. Archaic, forbidden, and very, very strong.

"What have you done?" Jag skimmed over the pages, the ancient language hard to decipher in a human's horrible handwriting. He moved his eyes from the page to the human. "What spell did you use?"

"I ..." the human stammered, shaking its head. "I don't really know."

Jag inhaled slowly, summoning patience, which was not his strongest attribute. "You had to have something in mind when you read an ancient tome written in blood, human."

"Jesus Christ," the human exhaled. "Th-that's real? That's blood and ..."

"What the hell did you think it was?" Jag lifted the book, clearly made of leathered skin and smelling of death, corruption, and magic. "Does this look like a normal book to you?"

"I didn't know it was real!"

Jag narrowed his eyes. "Then why did you *read* from it?"

The human flapped its mouth again and gave a helpless shrug. "For shiggles?"

"Use English!"

"How do you even KNOW English?" The human waved a hand at Jag, its voice pitched into hysterics. "How is any of this happening?"

Useless. The human was bloody useless.

Jag huffed out a frustrated breath and sheathed his sword to free up his other hand. Holding the flesh-bound book of blood magic, he began hunting for anything in the text that made sense. Jag was terrible at magic; it was not something in which a warrior was trained. This sort of cowardice, this dark magic, was outlawed hundreds of years ago. Demons would cross into other realms and manipulate weaker beings to do their bidding.

That was not allowed without permission from much higher-level demons. And probably a permit.

He knew very little about the forces that controlled this tome and the power it held, but he was tangled in them now. Stolen from his realm, his world, and thrown into that of beings whom he considered fodder at best.

What a waste of a day.

Jag rubbed his forehead to fight back the threatening headache, his skin tingling at the presence of human eyes on him. His gaze lifted to the human, who was standing again, its green eyes roaming over Jag in awe. Its skin was starting to take on a more pinkish hue, no longer a ghostly, ashen white. Its garments were odd, as was the creature itself. No armor, of course, only a large, heavy torso covering with a painted spear on it, and cloth pants decorated with white blobs wearing hats.

"Are you …" the human licked its lips, seeming to need to work up the courage to continue. "Are you a demon?"

"Yes." Jag puffed out his chest. "I'm Jagmarith of the Bone-reaver Clan."

"Wow. Demons have clans? I thought you all just worked for Satan." The human paled again. "Are you going to eat my soul?"

Jag barked out a laugh. He'd heard that humans had legends and myths about his kind, but the one about souls was by and large his favorite.

"No, human. I don't want your soul." Jag snickered. "I'm no sorcerer."

The human nodded but didn't seem very convinced. "Um … good. Good." The green eyes were at it again, studying him like

Jag was a mythical beast. "You don't have hooves or a tail. But wow ... those horns! They're really amazing."

Jag reached up and touched his horns out of reflex. No one had called his horns *amazing* before. He had always been very proud of his horns, but asking for praise for them would seem weak, like asking someone to notice how well his bones looked. A warrior didn't need to be vain.

Still, it felt nice.

"And your skin," the human continued. "It's such a unique color. It's not a bright, cartoon red! It's like blood red. But your eyes, that's ..." It paused and made a whistle noise with its mouth. "Like staring into the mouth of a volcano."

Jag couldn't help but blink as the human leaned forward, staring right into his eyes. Everyone in his clan had eyes like his. They weren't special at all. Not like the human's eyes, which were the same deep green as emeralds.

The human held out its hand, its palm out and slanted to the side. "I'm Ethan. Ethan of Clan ... Montgomery."

Jag glanced at its hand and squinted. "What are you doing?"

"It's a greeting? Do you not ... shake hands? Or ... should I bow or something?"

Humans really were clueless apes.

Jag sighed deeply and closed the book, setting it down on the machine that was rolling linen inside of it.

"The greetings are different depending on what your status is," Jag explained to the poor dumb human. "I would greet a fellow warrior in my clan differently than I would a stranger. What is your profession?"

"Me?" Ethan pointed at itself. "I'm a linguist. I study language."

"A scholar, then." Jag placed the fingers of his left hand to the wrist of his right, curling his right hand into a fist. "You would greet me as a scholar would a warrior. Like this."

The human studied him a moment, mirroring his greeting. "Like this?"

It was sloppy, but it was only human. "Yes. That's fine."

Ethan smiled, the action causing a glow to radiate from its entire being. The flush of pink against its cheeks made its eyes bright, and Jag felt his heart thump against his chest. The human had gone from being a wormy ape to a ray of sunshine in an instant. It was then that Jag truly drank in the image of Ethan of Clan Montgomery, scholar of languages in Earth realm.

Ethan was male, Jag could tell by his build, which was much smaller than Jag himself. Standing at his full height, the top of Ethan's curls came to the middle of Jag's chest. The tug of attraction surprised Jag since he was rarely one to have such sensations. There had been passing warriors, connections made and gone over his lifetime, but he had never thought anyone could *glow* quite like Ethan.

Jag cleared his throat, tearing his attention away from Ethan and back to the matter at hand. He needed to return to his keep and his own realm before things became more confusing and complicated. He reached for the book. A siren blasted from the machine as soon as his hand got close to it. Jag hissed through his teeth, jerking his hand back to the hilt of his sword.

"Whoa, whoa!" Ethan stepped around Jag and held up his hand. "It's my dryer. Nothing to be afraid of."

"I fear no manner of creature or machine, human," Jag corrected quickly, perhaps a touch more defensive than he needed to be. "But I will cut down anything that stands in the way of my getting home."

"That's fair." Ethan gave the machine a pat. "But this isn't standing in your way. It was just letting me know it's done drying."

"The sound was foul—" Jag felt a surge of magic ripple through the air, the smell and tingle of its presence familiar. He tightened his fingers around his sword and placed himself in front of the invading magic, ready to cut it down. Had something followed him through the human-made gate? Another demon, perhaps?

Friend or foe, Jagmarith was ready to fight.

Ethan peeked around Jag, seeming confused and oblivious to the swirling in the air. Not a heartbeat later, a crack formed in the space in front of them, reality peeling away like a fresh wound oozing with black and green light. Ethan gave a shout and ducked away and Jag stepped forward, readying himself.

"Show yourself!" Jag demanded.

"Master!" Sami's voice echoed through the crack before he slid through, waving his hand to dismiss the fissure. The crack between the realms sealed back up and vanished, the ripple fading. "Are you okay, Master?"

"Sami." Jag relaxed his fingers, breathing out a slow breath of relief. "How did you find me?"

"I can always find you, Master." Sami glanced around, his hands resting on his hips. The small familiar twitched his pointy ears, his long nose flaring as he breathed in the air. "Hmm. Looks like a basement."

"Wow." Ethan inched around Jag to study Sami. "Are you a demon too?"

Sami bared his needle teeth and hissed, flattening his ears down on his skull like an angry cat. Ethan squeaked in alarm, and Jag lifted his palm.

"Easy, Sami. This is Ethan of Clan Montgomery. He's a scholar of languages."

Sami lifted his ears and closed his mouth. "Oh. Hi, Ethan."

"Uh ... hi?" Ethan waved a little, then remembering his previous lesson, greeted Sami with the completely wrong motion. Sami blinked, sliding his inky eyes to Jag in surprise.

Jag shook his head. "He's very bad at greetings."

Sami nodded in understanding, sympathy for the poor human in his eyes.

"No time to waste." Jag adjusted his scabbard and motioned

towards where Sami had sealed the fissure between realms. "Open the door back up so we can go back, Sami. We cannot leave my keep defenseless."

"Master, a demon cannot travel between realms in a familiar's portal. My magic isn't strong enough to support you." His pointy ears slanted down in sorrow. "Only demon magic can send you home."

Of fucking course. Nothing could be simple when it came to magic. One of the many reasons why Jag hated it so much. Jag gave the machine with linens a glare before he snatched the book from its top, passing it over to Sami.

"This is what Ethan read from before I arrived. Can you make sense of it?"

Shock widened Sami's large black eyes as he took the book carefully with both of his clawed hands. He opened the pages, his mouth opening in a silent breath of awe, and Jag could see the reflection of the blood lettering in his massive eyes.

"Blood magic! These books are so rare!" Sami's black pools darted to Ethan, hope shining in them. "Where did you get this?"

Ethan's cheeks heated, sending splotches down his neck as he rubbed the back of his head. "I ... sort of ... slightly stole it?"

That was surprising. Jag looked at the human, lifting an eyebrow.

"What!" Ethan shrugged his shoulders up. "The university wasn't using it! It's winter break. No one is there. I thought I could get a little extra research in. I was gonna give it back ..." he trailed off, the splotches on his neck getting bright.

Sami hummed as he carefully flipped through the pages of the book, eyes scanning the script. "There are all types of incantations and summoning spells in here. Each one of these is a different gateway between our realms, pathways with very specific conditions. How you get home depends heavily on which of these he used, Master."

Jag scrubbed a hand over his face, frustration spiking his

blood pressure. "I hate magic. Ethan, which spell did you use to summon me?"

Ethan skirted around Jag, giving Sami a wide berth as he travelled to the other side of the room and gathered up a flimsy book with wires for the spine. His dark brows knitted together as he scanned the handwriting inside, penned in ink rather than blood.

"I've been trying to translate and understand the language in that book for about a year and a half," Ethan explained. "So, this might not be exactly right. But from what I understand, I read something about a promise or a wish, maybe? Something about muscles or maybe organs?"

Sami tilted his head. "Oath of the Heart?"

"Oath! Yes!" Ethan lit up again with excitement, his smile almost blinding. "I need to write this down. I've been working on this for so long!"

Sami inhaled through his teeth. "That's not good."

"Why?" Jag scowled. "What does that mean? What is an Oath of the Heart?"

While Ethan scribbled away on his paper, Sami's ears flattened as he aimed worried eyes toward his master.

"Some of these spells are like invitations," Sami explained, flapping his hands around as he often did, mimicking opening a door and inviting someone inside. "A way for a human to usher a demon into the realm to visit. Normally there's a time limit on the invite, a fail-safe to make sure the demon can't outstay their welcome."

Sami placed his wrists together like they were shackled. "Some of them are binding summons. They're not invitations, but more like kidnapping. These are spells used to pluck up demons unwillingly and force them to do a human's bidding, or else they'll be stuck here under their control."

Jag set his jaw, his molars grinding. "This wasn't the inviting one, I assume."

Sami swallowed. "No, Master. It wasn't. An Oath of the Heart has very strict rules. You must do exactly what Ethan wants, or you'll be stuck in this realm forever."

"Why did you summon me?" Jag glared at the cowering human. "What are your terms, Ethan?"

"I don't have any!" Ethan held up his palms. "Seriously, I didn't mean to bring you here! You're dismissed!" He swept his hands forward like he was wiping a table clean. "I hereby release you! You're free from the oath!"

"It doesn't work that way." Sami's voice sounded weak and sad, like his whole being was shrinking in on itself. "The oath is only released once the conditions are met."

"But I didn't list any conditions!" Ethan shook his head, his curls bouncing. "I don't have any!"

Sami tapped himself across his sternum. "It's an oath of the *heart*. What was in your heart when you read the passage?"

"Blood, mostly." Ethan laughed at his own joke, quickly quieting when no one else joined him. "Well, I guess I'm ..." he trailed off, the splotches resurfacing.

"Go on," Sami coaxed, rotating his hand in a wheel motion. "Do you need revenge? Someone dismembered? Master Jagmarith is very good at that."

"Jesus! No." Ethan ran his fingers through his curls, sending them into a wild, fizzy mess. "I've been stressed over seeing my ex-fiancée tomorrow at a holiday party. That's been on my mind all week."

Jag exhaled, understanding. "So you need me to slaughter him."

"No!"

"Flay him?" Sami offered. "Disembowel him? Oh, Master, you can break in your new bone extracting knife!"

Jag pondered, tapping his chin. "Could you bring that to me through the rift?"

Sami nodded quickly, clearly happy to help.

"None of that! No horrible torturing or ... *bone extracting!*"

Ethan sounded panicked, his voice pitched higher than it was when the conversation began. "I don't want him dead or hurt. I just want to make him jealous."

"Jealous ... that you have skin and he doesn't?" Sami asked, confused.

"No, I think he means jealous that Ethan still has eyes," Jag corrected.

"Oh my God." Ethan placed his hands together and inhaled slowly. "I mean more like show up with a really hot date. He sees me walk in with some hunk and realizes that he dumped someone who could land a supermodel or a bodybuilder."

"Then why did you summon a demon?" Jag wrinkled his nose.

"I didn't mean to." Ethan let his arms drop in defeat. "I didn't think reading from the book would work. From what I under-stood of my translation, it sounded like ..." he paused and sighed. "It was more likely a demon would come to my rescue then me actually landing a date."

"Surely there are human suitors for you to choose from." Jag motioned to Ethan with his hand. "You seem healthy. Are scholars not held in high regards on Earth?" He thought about what he knew about humans and bobbed his head in acknowl-edgment. "Maybe not, actually. You do seem to burn people alive for speaking about science."

Ethan laughed, the sound a golden light in the dim basement. It was pleasing.

"I'm not popular with the guys, no." Ethan rubbed at his neck, emerald eyes downcast.

"Master." Sami wrung his hands together. "I believe this means that you'll need to accompany Ethan to this event as his date for the evening."

It was Jag's turn to laugh because that notion was hysterically outlandish. "Good one, Sami. Your comedy routine is getting much better."

"Thank you, Master, but I'm being serious."

The humor started to fade as Jag looked between his familiar and the emerald-eyed human. Jagmarith was no suitor. He was a warrior, Champion of the Blood Wars, collector of his enemies' skulls, and wearer of his clan's armor. He was *not* a tool in a petty squabble between a heartbroken human and his former lover.

"It would be easier to just kill him," Jag muttered to himself. "How am I supposed to go out into the human world like this anyway? I'll strike fear into the hearts of these wormy humans."

"You're not allowed to expose your demon self, Master. Not without a permit." Sami wrung his hands together. "But I can help you disguise yourself as a human while in this realm."

Jag motioned for him to continue, a headache brewing from annoyance. Small green hands went to work crafting something with magic, tiny electric sparks floating into the air as he knitted an amulet together. The round spiral had a crest of deception at its center, tethered with two straps of black leather so it could be worn around someone's neck.

"Here you are, Master." Sami grinned, showing his rows of baby shark teeth. "A simple charm of deception. Powerful enough for humans to be fooled."

Jag accepted the amulet, feeling its weight and the tingle of magic across his palm. He'd never had to take any form but his own, never relied on magic on the battlefield. A small pinch of uneasiness nipped into his gut as he slipped the necklace over his head, but he'd be damned if cowardice would sway him now.

It was only a minor spell. Nothing to scare Jagmarith.

The air around them shifted again, the magic swelling around his feet and slithering over his skin. Dark tendrils snaked around him, burrowing into his flesh and worming around just below the surface. Jag flexed his fingers and shook his limbs in a desperate attempt to knock the magic loose. His crimson skin began to melt into a different color, morphing to a tawny beige before his eyes.

His form began to shrink, his bones contracting as his horns receded back into his skull. Jag shouted, reaching up to try and grab his proud demon horns before they could disappear, only to feel them slip back beneath the skin. As the final insult to injury, his armor became loose around his shoulders and hips, his muscle mass shrinking just enough to cause his legacy to slip out of place.

Jag traced the place his horns had been, the shoulders of his armor clacking as he moved. His sword dipped, too heavy now for his narrow waist, and the tip touched the ground.

"Satan's horns ..." Jag whispered, his voice softer than it once was. "What has become of me?"

Ethan made a strangled noise in his throat. Sami covered his mouth with both hands to suppress a scream.

Jag looked down at himself again, still pained by what he saw. His armor was loose around his form, which was the wrong color for his species. His skull seemed so much lighter without his mighty horns, and he felt naked without them. Finding smooth skin where his horns once were made him ache.

"I'm disgusting."

"No, Master, no!" Sami shook his head, but his ears were pressed back. He was a terrible liar, most familiars were. "You look ... less wormy than most humans! Mighty even! Right, Ethan?"

Ethan made a squeaky noise that wasn't helpful.

This situation was not ideal. It was close to nightmarish. Jag had never felt so small and pathetic in his life, his armor offensively loose around him. The urge to rip the charm off his neck and choke someone with it was almost unbearable. Having to parade around as a human even for a moment was degrading.

What choice did he have?

It was either swallow his pride and do as the oath required, or he'd be stuck as a hornless, small human for the rest of his days. Jagmarith would not allow such dishonor to himself and his clan.

Jag puffed out his chest and held his belt in place. "When is this party?"

"Tomorrow night," Ethan said carefully, his eyes unsure and worried.

"Sami," Jag turned to his trusted familiar, who gave him a salute. "Go home and guard the keep while I'm gone."

"Are you sure you don't want me to stay, Master? I can help navigate their customs for you."

"No, I can't leave my keep vulnerable. Besides," Jag nodded to Ethan. "He'll fill me in on what I need to know."

"Yes, Master." Sami gave another salute and made a wide gesture with his hands, tearing open a gateway like he had before. The tear between realms rippled and blinked with magic, opening just wide enough for the tiny familiar. "I'll come check on you after the party."

Jag nodded and his familiar slipped away, the tear sealing behind him.

Silence hung in the air between Jag and Ethan, the human nervously plucking at the hem of his sweater.

"Are you hungry?" Ethan lifted his brows. "Do you eat?"

"Yes, I eat." Jag adjusted a shoulder pauldron sliding out of place. "I need garments more suitable for this form."

"Oh, sure." Ethan jumped into action, moving to the stack of cardboard boxes leaning against the wall. He sifted through a couple of them, picking through clothing and holding them up to inspect. After a couple of shuffles, he came back to Jag with an armful of clothing. "You're pretty big, so I'm not sure if these will fit you. But it's the best I have at the moment."

Jag grabbed the thing on top of the pile and lifted it up. It was a thick torso covering like Ethan's, but instead of being decorated with a spear, it was solid black with white lettering.

"What is 'Hollister'? Is this a clan?"

Ethan bit his lower lip with a smile and shook his head. "Just a clothing brand."

Even in his smaller human form, Jag still stood much taller than Ethan. Jag had shrunk more in mass than height, and Ethan had to angle his head up to reach Jag's eyes. Jag gave a sigh and detached his armor, slipping out of it so he could change into human clothing.

Ethan's eyes shot up to the ceiling as Jag stripped nude, the human's cheeks heating up again for some reason.

The clothing did not fit well. The torso covering was tight around his arms and only came to his navel. The cloth pants with the matching Hollister clan name weren't much better. He looks ridiculous.

"This is foolish," Jag snarled, pulling the clinging garment loose after it tucked itself too snuggly against his ass.

"It's the best I have for now. You definitely can't fit into anything I own." Ethan shrugged helplessly. "We can go shopping tomorrow and get you something for the party."

"If these aren't yours, then who is part of Clan Hollister?" Jag plucked the cloth against his chest.

"Those are David's. My ex." Ethan tossed the clothing Jag hadn't picked back in the boxes. "C'mon. Let's get some dinner. What do demons eat, exactly?"

Jag followed Ethan up the stairs, the upper floor revealing much more of the domicile. It was a small building, nothing like the keeps Jag was used to back home. The construction was mostly wood and brick, painted over in various shades of cream and dark blue. The floor was furry and soft, creaking as they moved through different rooms. The walls had pictures under glass, Ethan in many of them, but some showing humans Jag did not know.

The air in the home was pleasant. It smelled like roasted meat and root vegetables, with a much more subtle scent of cleaner and linen. Stuffed furniture or wooden tables with chairs seemed to be in every room, giving guests and family plenty of places to sit and relax. Jag did not note a single blade on display or any armor showcased, which was puzzling. He wondered what sort of clan the Montgomery's were.

"Where is the rest of your clan?" Jag followed Ethan into the kitchen, the furry floor giving way to dark, cold stone. On the counter, a large pot was plugged into an outlet, bubbling with the source of the wonderful smell.

"It's just me here." Ethan pulled ceramic bowls from a cabinet. "My parents passed away five years ago and I inherited the house. My sister lives in Portland, so it's just me."

"Do you still have their armor? Or were they scholars like you?"

Ethan blinked up at Jag, surprise on his face. "Oh, um … my mom was a scholar. A teacher of history. My dad was a technician. He worked on internet networks and …" he paused as Jag scrunched up his face in confusion. "Um, he was a sorcerer. Not this type of magic, obviously, but the human kind."

"Ah." Jag nodded. "Noble professions. What exactly do you do besides read from dangerous books?"

Ethan choked on a laugh that seemed to be stuck in his nose. "I'm a linguist. Well, I'm an assistant professor at the moment working on my PhD. My job is to mostly help grade papers, but I read from dangerous books on the side."

Ethan uncovered the stew, stirring it with a ladle before scooping out a large bowl for each of them. It smelled amazing, the spices and meat causing Jag's stomach to rumble in anticipation.

"Careful, it's probably really hot—oh, ok." Ethan could barely get his words out before Jag was drinking from the bowl, consuming the stew in great mouthfuls. It was as delicious as it smelled, with tender bovine, acidic vegetables, roots, and spices he'd never had before. Sami had introduced him to some through his experimental human cuisine, but Ethan was much better at it.

Jag held out the bowl for more after he had finished and Ethan laughed in surprise.

"I guess that means you like it?" he asked as he scooped more into Jag's bowl. Jag nodded, eating more slowly this time.

Ethan leaned against the counter and ate his stew with a metal utensil, which seemed grueling to Jag. Each tiny scoop only held a couple bites of scrumptious food. It must have been some sort of self-inflicted suffering or discipline that Jag was unaware of. To make matters more torturous, Ethan had to blow on each bite to cool it before he could eat it.

Humans were such strange, fragile things.

"So." Ethan stirred his stew absently. "What's Hell like? Do you really have boiling lakes of fire and all that?"

"Oh, yes. The fire lakes are truly beautiful. I spent my childhood there during the summer months, fishing for ember fish."

There was a long pause as Ethan studied Jag's face, a line denting between his brows as he pondered what had been said. "You're serious."

"I'm always serious."

"You make it sound like a lake made of fire would be a pleasant experience."

"It is." Jag shrugged. "If you're a demon."

Musical laughter lifted from Ethan as he carried his empty bowl to the sink and rinsed it clean. He turned to Jag, drying the small ceramic bowl with a rag printed with odd, round-headed figures with dots down their midsections.

"Are there other species of demons besides what you are?"

"Hm." Jag crossed his arms as he leaned against the counter, kicking around how best to answer him without exposing too much. "Do you have one in particular you're curious about?"

"Well like ... what about Incubi?"

Jag glanced at the human, who was watching him closely. Ethan's emerald eyes had cast a spell on him that made Jag weak. Something was dancing in those jewels, and the way Ethan's pink lips worried against his teeth made Jag want to stroke his thumb against them.

Weakened over a tiny human. What would your clan think of you?

"Why do you want to know about Incubi?" Jag finally asked, unable to keep himself from indulging this little human's curiosities.

The flush of pink on Ethan's cheeks was starting to become an addiction to Jag.

"There was just this book series that I really liked that had Incubi in it." Ethan spun the bowl in his hand, wiping the cloth around it again even though it was bone dry. "And I wanted to know if they were real."

That piqued Jag's interest. He had always wondered if humans got demons correct in their stories.

"Tell me about them."

Ethan nearly dropped the bowl. "Tell you about the ... the series?"

"Yes. What did they look like? What were their powers? Why did you find them interesting?"

"Oh, they ... it was ..." he floundered, assaulting the bowl again with the rag. Jag wondered if he'd be peeling the coloring off the damn thing. "It was fiction, so it's probably wrong anyway."

"Tell me."

Ethan swallowed. "Well, they um ... they were really powerful demons who got their strength from sex. Like sex gave them energy they could wield and use to shift into these really hot guys with wings and horns--"

Jag's brows lifted, and Ethan made a squeak.

"So you are attracted to demons with horns who like sex?"

"Oh, man, it's getting so late!" Ethan hurled the bowl into the sink, stretching tall with a yawn. "We have a big day tomorrow, so I'm going to turn in. I'll show you to the guest room where you can sleep. You're probably so tired from being torn across realms, right? Ha-ha! What a day!"

Ethan abandoned the kitchen in a hurry, dashing out like the room was on fire.

Jag followed at a more leisurely pace, watching as Ethan stormed up the stairs, tripping halfway up. He slid back down sideways on his hip before crawling up the rest of the way like a terrified animal escaping a predator. It was quite the sight.

On the second floor of the small home, three rooms splintered off from the hallway, which was lined with more short fur. Older photographs were on the walls, including one of a clearly young Ethan with three other humans: an older female child and two adults. All of them wore long-sleeved garments like Ethan was wearing currently, fluffy and adorned with the same odd patterns. They all were smiling, the likeness of Ethan's eyes and nose pulled from either adult.

"These are your parents." Jag tapped the glass.

Ethan, much less skittish than he was while climbing the stairs, backtracked down the hallway to gaze at the picture.

"Yep. That's them and my sister."

"Are these traditional garments?" Jag eyed the clothing in the picture before looking back at Ethan, who gave a laugh.

"Yeah, kind of. We were really into Christmas around here." When Jag furrowed his brow in confusion, Ethan continued. "It's the winter holiday we celebrate. It's named after the Christian holiday celebrating Jesus's birthday; we're not religious, so it was more of a secular celebration. The party we're going to tomorrow is Christmas themed."

Jag growled at the mention of religion. Every system of worship since the beginnings of mankind had something in place to ward off his kind. Some had symbols, others ceremonies, a couple even found minerals in the earth that naturally repelled demons.

It was fucking frustrating, and something he wasn't equipped to handle in a human body.

But the holiday-themed things that Ethan claimed as his celebration were harmless; otherwise, Jag would have felt it the moment he arrived.

He shook himself free of his thoughts and looked to Ethan. "Where am I sleeping?"

"Oh, right. You'll take my sister's old room." Ethan glanced at the picture one more time, something distant in his gaze, before leading Jag down the hallway. It was clear that the bedroom hadn't been touched in some time, the small bed perfectly made, items left untouched long enough to have a fine layer of dust around the base.

Spread across the wooden dresser, an arrangement of stuffed toys and soulless dolls stared forward with unblinking marble eyes. Jag shuddered.

"I'd offer you my old room, but I turned it into an office." Ethan clicked on a lamp beside the bed, the soft light giving just enough illumination to warm the small room. "Sorry about the creepy dolls. But they probably don't freak you out, huh?"

Jag shook his head but narrowed his eyes at the doll in the pink, frilly dress; it was staring at him. He hated that one the most.

Ethan paused in the doorway. "Goodnight, Jag."

Jag flicked his eyes to Ethan, not wanting to take his eyes off the doll too long. "Goodnight, Ethan."

Before he took to the small bed to get some rest, Jag banished the dolls to the closet to help ease his discomfort. He checked that the door was shut tight before crawling into bed. The mattress was soft but a little stiff and his feet hung off the end. The linen sheets and pillowcases smelled of faded floral soap that was pleasant.

As Jag double-checked that the closet was still shut, he felt exhaustion pulling him into sleep.

Jagmarith, second son of Bolor'gath, Champion of the Blood Wars, and carrier of his clan's armor, had no idea what was in store for him.

2

THE GREAT DEMON BAKING SHOW

The smell of cooking meat pulled Jag out of his slumber.

His human body was stiff and awkward as he climbed out of the tiny bed, shuffling out of the room to find a place to relieve himself. The bathroom was a door down, softly lit by the sleepy morning sun. Jag was happy to learn that his proportions were still correct as he drained his bladder into the ceramic toilet, worried that his shrinking size had affected *every* part of him.

It had not. And it made him grin.

What was less satisfying was seeing his human face staring back at him in the mirror hanging over the sink. He barely recognized himself. All of his facial features remained true, the size of his eyes, the shape of his nose, mouth, and chin, but it was the rest that shook him. He'd never seen himself without horns before, never seen his ears rounded.

Even his eyes were wrong.

No longer were they churning lava red with golden centers, but a bright shade of amber with a dark ring around the edges. His cheeks and jaw were growing dark stubble which was rough against his palm.

Jag tugged his long hair down from the tight bun, thankful the dark locks remained the same. The one thing he was able to keep that was his own. Running his fingers through it made him feel better, much less hideous as a pale, wormy human.

Downstairs, the sizzle of meat in a metal pan made Jag's stomach roar to life. From the small speaker on the kitchen counter, upbeat, jingly melodies played, the lyrics touting celebrations about winter, snow, and reindeer with odd facial abnormalities.

"Good morning." Ethan turned with a smile, his eyes widening for a moment. "Your hair."

Jag gathered his beloved hair into his hands and scowled. "What about my hair?"

"It's pretty." Ethan's face paled before flushing red, his eyes bugging out. "I mean manly! Manly. Good. Manly, good hair."

Jag pointed. "Your pan is on fire."

Ethan cursed and moved the pan off the burner, easing the smoke and throwing away the burnt strips of meat.

"There's coffee if you want any," he said over his shoulder as he placed fresh strips of meat into the pan. "I'll scramble some eggs to go with the bacon."

Sami had made Jag coffee before, and he remembered liking the bitter taste. He poured himself some of the black liquid, sipping on it with a happy hum.

"After breakfast, I'm going to run to the store and get the supplies I need for baking today. I'll also get you some clothes that actually fit." Ethan cracked some eggs into a large bowl, whisking it with milk and spices.

"What are you cooking after this?" Jag watched him pour the egg mixture into another pan, his movements comfortable and relaxed.

"I have so many things to make before the party." He pushed the eggs around with one hand, the other flipping strips of meat. It was very impressive. "I'm making cookies, pie, peanut butter balls, and maybe some reindeer bait."

"You're going hunting?" Jag perked up.

"Oh—no. That's what this treat is called. It's salty snacks covered in white chocolate. It's really good." Ethan placed the cooked meat strips onto a plate lined with paper, then scooped warm, fluffy eggs onto two plates. He plucked some toasted bread from a machine and tossed them onto each egg plate, divided the meat strips, and handed Jag a plate.

Jag picked up a strip of cooked meat and took a bite; the crisp of the meat made him shut his eyes in happiness.

"You are an amazing cook," Jag said between bites of meat.

"It's just eggs and bacon. Nothing special," Ethan said humbly as he handed Jag a metal utensil.

"Sami has tried to make this for me before. The eggs were rubbery and the bacon was floppy and disgusting. This is truly delicious."

Ethan didn't respond the second time, but Jag noticed the rose coloring in his cheeks. Jag continued to eat as Ethan finished up his food, washing the plate off with water before putting it into a machine. He made his way into the connecting room, turning on an electronic device with a screen as Jag walked in to see it.

"I'll be back in a couple of hours." Ethan handed him a small plastic object that apparently controlled the electronic screen. Jag glanced down at the object, only having a vague idea of what it did, and pushed some of the buttons to learn what they did. It didn't take long to discover which ones controlled the volume, changed what was playing on the screen, or simply shut the whole thing off.

Jag munched on his food as Ethan slipped on a big coat and left, leaving the house quiet beyond the noise coming out of the television. Most of the channels Jag landed on were advertisements, documentaries about old murders, a couple of competition shows with giant wheels, and other nonsense.

He was about to turn it off when he landed on a channel claiming to be streaming holiday movies all day, Christmas movies in particular. Jag considered this to be a prime research opportunity and settled in to learn all he could about this holiday while Ethan was gone.

In the handful of hours watching movies in Ethan's absence, Jag was able to learn a couple of things about Christmas.

One, humans had a tendency to haul large trees into their homes and throw lights on them. This was never explained.

Two, Santa is worshiped and given offerings of cookies in exchange for gifts. It was unclear what happens if cookies aren't left, but there had been mention of coal. From what Jag could infer, Santa turned children into coal for misbehaving. No longer in danger of Santa's wrath, the parents often teased the children about their possible fate.

Three, people gathered around the light trees and opened gifts, which seemed to solve most of the problems they were having. Santa was truly a generous deity when his anger was sated.

Four, humans were not scared of snow, and they should be.

Jag was finishing a movie about a man trapped in a corporate building, fighting terrorists, when Ethan came home. His arms were packed with bags, packages of chocolate and containers clattering to the ground as he tried to place it all on the counters. Jag jumped up to assist, catching a bag filled with flour, a carton of eggs, and other things before it crashed to the ground.

"I don't know why in the hell I thought it was a good idea to do this on Christmas Eve, but I got most everything I needed," Ethan said with a huff, digging in the bags to unpack them. "I have so much to do before tonight."

"I can assist." Jag followed Ethan's lead, pulling items out of bags and lining them across the counter.

Ethan blinked. "You ... want to help me bake?"

"I'd rather be productive than sit any longer."

Happiness shone in Ethan's eyes as he smiled, lighting up the room. "Great! I'll put you on cookie-decorating duty."

Jag felt his chest fill with swarms of bugs, his heart floating amidst the invasion. "I will do my very best."

Just like with the meal he had prepared earlier, Ethan moved around the kitchen with confidence and grace. Jag was enamored of the speed and agility the human had when it came to food preparation. Most of his tasks were done while juggling several different tasks: melting chocolate, prepping dough, whisking, filling, and so on. Flour dusted his arms and there was even a little on his face, a melody humming from his lips as he worked.

Jag recognized the tune as one of the odd songs played over the speaker. This one was about visiting a relative who lived in the woods.

Ethan grabbed a club with a handle on each end and used the weapon to smooth out cookie dough on a large, flat surface. Jag enjoyed how his forearms flexed as he worked, his garment—a "sweater" is what it was called in one of the movies—pushed up to his elbows.

"What I need you to do is take these cookie cutters and press them through the dough, then transfer the cutouts onto the pan." Ethan grabbed a metal object in the shape of a barbed spear and pressed it into the dough. The metal sliced through the dough with ease, and Ethan carefully lifted the cutout and placed it on a metal sheet.

Jag nodded, rolling up his short sleeves. "I can do that."

Ethan handed Jag his selection of cutters and stepped around him to work on another project.

The objects were all different, and Jag mused over what they could be. There was the spear, of course, a circle with a cap, a rounded human with no fingers or toes, and a bent line with a curved hook. All very strange, but he didn't question it. Jag was as careful as he could be with his large hands honed for war, tearing a couple of the floppy dough cutouts while cursing under his breath.

They were so tiny and fragile. It was frustrating.

Once he arranged them on the sheet, Ethan slid the pan into the oven to bake, giving Jag the task of dipping rolled balls in chocolate. It was insanely messy, and Ethan laughed at how much of the melted, sweet substance had made it onto Jag instead of the peanut butter balls.

"I'm not adept to this task," Jag growled, fingers sticky with sugar, flour from the cookies dusting his sweater.

"You're doing great." Ethan came over with a warm, wet towel and captured one of Jag's hands, scrubbing the chocolate off of it. "I've never had an assistant before. It's cutting my work in half."

"I've mangled some of the balls." Jag glared at the offensive blobs of goop he'd tried to craft. "And torn some of the cookies. I don't think I'm helping."

"They don't have to be perfect." Ethan's eyes danced as he smiled, and Jag felt a little better about everything. "They just need to taste good. Why don't you try one out and let me know how they are?"

Jag plucked up one of the ugly monstrosities he had crafted and popped it into his mouth, chomping down on the warm, soft dessert. He'd never had peanut butter and chocolate before, and he was fairly sure he'd never taste anything so wonderful again.

"Sweet Satan's shadow," Jag muttered in the throes of sugary bliss.

"Good?" Ethan's eyebrows were raised, his smile on the edge between amused and worried.

"This is the best thing I've ever put in my mouth."

Ethan coughed and caught a dish he almost knocked over. "That's ... great! Great."

A timer went off, spurring Ethan into action. He removed the tray of cookies from the oven, the smell of the tiny baked goods warming the air. Jag watched as Ethan transferred the little shapes off the hot pan and onto a cool surface.

"Once these are all cool, we'll use the icing and sprinkles to decorate them. I'll make one as a template for you."

"How did you learn to craft such delicacies?" Jag managed around his bite of bliss.

A pie was slipped into the oven and another timer set. "My mom used to bake like crazy during the holidays. I learned a lot of this stuff from her." Ethan wiped his hands on his apron, which was smeared with flour and dried chocolate. "Do demons have parents? Family?"

Jag tore his eyes away from the tempting peanut butter balls, wanting to devour all of them. "Yes. My mother is a great warrior who led a slaughter against the rival clans. My brother is an architect."

"Oh. Wow." Ethan blinked, clearly impressed. "Wasn't expecting architect."

"Do you normally bake this much?" Jag waved his hand over the spread. "I've seen how much you eat. This would last you a while."

"I always bake this much for the holiday party." Ethan's smile faltered. "Since my sister lives far away and my parents are gone, the party is my family gathering. It's all of the good friends that I've known a long time."

"And your ex," Jag added, thinking perhaps Ethan had forgotten. By the wince that pinched Ethan's face, he had not.

"And my ex." A long, heavy sigh escaped from him, his shoulders sagging. "That's the downside of being dumped by a guy you dated for four years. You often have the same friends."

"Dumped? He forsook you?" Jag was dumbfounded. "Why?"

"He said it was because we grew apart, but I think he just wanted to date someone else." Ethan's shrug was halfhearted and broken. "I'm not as exciting as a travelling journalist with a six pack."

"He's a fool."

That brought more glow to Ethan's face as a smile crept back into place. "Um, I think the cookies are cool." Ethan tested the surface of the cookies with his fingers before sliding over several colorful containers.

Jag made his way over to the cookies, standing beside Ethan as he explained the process of icing the tiny baked goods. The thick, sugar-based paint came in all shades, from bone white to coal black, blood red, and acid green, and even a pleasant poison blue that Jag liked. Small sugar beads and oblong crystals were available for "accents," but Jag had no idea what that meant.

Ethan smeared a circle cookie with white icing, then packed other colors into tubes he then squeezed out in fine lines. His sugar-painting skills were very impressive, and soon the plain, round cookie was sparkling with sprinkles and multicolored lines.

"You have enormous faith in my painting abilities if you want me to make that." Jag pointed at the masterpiece. "Mine will be terrible."

"They don't have to be perfect, Jag," Ethan said around a smile, handing Jag a clean knife to spread on the icing. "Decorate them however you want. I'm sure they'll be beautiful no matter what."

It warmed Jag to know that Ethan trusted him with such an important task. These treats were going to his family, or people he considered family, and it was up to Jag to make sure they looked nice. The lumpy, monstrous peanut butter balls he had helped dip were not the best representation of Jag's potential. He could do better.

No.

He *would* do better.

I have conquered much worse trials. Slain armies, won wars, carried the honor of my clan into battle.

He would not fail.

The first four cookies were grotesque failures on his part of understanding the consistency of the icing and sprinkles. Jag had attempted to make lines like Ethan had, only to learn the hard way that squeezing the tube too hard caused a volcanic eruption out of both ends. Blood red icing coated a circle and a round human, and Jag stared in absolute horror as Ethan laughed.

Sprinkles coated the workspace, mocking Jag with how badly they stuck to everything *except* his cookies. The audacity of the tiny sugar flakes made his blood boil.

By the fifth or sixth cookie, Jag had a much better grip on the process. He hadn't quite mastered the artistic grace of Ethan's example, but Jag was able to reign in the icing enough to at least attempt designs. At cookie number eight, he was very confident in his skills and set out to make the best damn cookie possible. Jag carefully placed lines just so, adding dashes of glittery sprinkles and well-placed candies for added effect.

He had been so consumed in his latest masterpiece that he hadn't noticed Ethan standing next to him until Jag unfolded from his perch. His back popped as he stretched his arms forward, having been bent over the cookie sheet while he crafted tiny works of art.

Ethan's pretty eyes were wide as he scanned over Jag's work, his mouth open in surprise.

"Those are ... unique," Ethan offered carefully. "Are those Christmas trees bleeding?"

"Trees?" Jag glanced between Ethan and his work. "Aren't they spears?"

"Sure. They can be spears." Ethan nodded slowly. "Glittery, bloody spears. And that gingerbread man is ..."

"Decapitated."

"Naturally." Ethan put his hands on his hips. "The piping on the pentagram ornaments is really good."

Jag beamed.

"We have a little time before the party." Ethan pulled his phone from his pocket and checked the time. "We should probably get cleaned up. I'll let you use the shower first if you want. Oh! And I got you some clothes." He tossed his apron across a chair and grabbed a plastic bag filled with garments. "I went a couple sizes up from what you're wearing now. They should fit."

The plastic bag was stuffed with folded items Jag didn't recognize, the materials unfamiliar to a demon. Jag reached in and touched the fabric carefully as he followed Ethan toward the bathing area. A couple of the items were very soft, made with wide threads in different dark colors.

Back upstairs, Ethan led Jag to a bathroom that had a standing shower stall. The knobs above the faucet controlled the temperature of the water, never quite getting hot enough for his skin. The soap available for Jag to use smelled like sticks and earth; another bottle, for his hair, smelled like citrus.

It was very pleasant.

Ethan left Jag alone while he bathed in disappointingly mild water, scrubbing his human skin clean. The amount of chocolate and flour on him after only an afternoon of decorating was surprising, and Jag wondered if humans were naturally sticky.

Once he was clean, Jag pulled the clothing from the bag and examined his options. The rougher fabric was a pair of pants in a dark blue shade. They fit, though they limited his range of motion. How in hell did humans fight in these? They were tight against his backside in a way that would make kicking impossible.

There had been a package of shorts that seemed to go under the pants, but Jag skipped those. He wasn't sure of their purpose. While sorting through his sweater options, one in particular caught his attention. Unlike the other sweater, which was black and plain, the one at the bottom was similar to the ones Ethan and his clan wore in the picture he had noticed.

The thick fabric was bright red with black, stitched designs of chains, bats, and ornate patterns around the arms. In the center, a crude depiction of a demon carrying away a child in a sack was displayed, with the words "Merry Krampus" just below it.

The Krampus sweater was very soft and fit well, and Jag

couldn't help but run his hand over it as he walked back to the kitchen. Ethan beamed when he saw Jag, a laugh bubbling up from him as his cheeks flushed.

"You actually wore it!"

"I like it." Jag pulled the fabric forward so he could view the Krampus Demon again. "He's carrying away a child. It amuses me."

"It looks really good on you." The pink around Ethan's neck got blotchy again. "I-I mean the color. Cause it's red and you're red. Well, not *right now* but usually you're red, so it looks good?"

Jag stared. "What?"

"Gotta shower!" Ethan spun on his heels and ran out of the kitchen, nearly tripping over the divide between rooms as he scurried away.

In his absence, Jag ate three more peanut butter balls and caught the first half of a holiday movie he hadn't seen yet. This particular tale was about a human living among the enslaved elves of Santa's lair. The human was visiting the Earth realm, discovering things unknown to him in a quest to find his father. Jag could relate to the human-elf's confusion and was glad he didn't have to visit New York.

It seemed ... crowded.

When Ethan returned from upstairs, he was no longer covered in flour and smears of chocolate. His skin smelled like the wash Jag had used, but somehow it was delicious coming from him. The scent on Jag was like sticks and earth, but on Ethan it was a fresh forest to explore. The citrus coming from his hair was sweet, and Jag felt an odd sensation where his horns once were. He touched the spot absently as he reeled himself in.

Ethan had also changed clothing, sporting a new, loud sweater with a reindeer in the center, its nose blinking red with a small light. He seemed very proud of it. Jag also couldn't help but notice how well Ethan's pants fit him. There apparently was a trend about human pants fitting snugly around the backside.

Jag had been so captivated by the lovely view that he hadn't realized Ethan had been talking.

"What?"

Ethan had a faint smile on his lips that almost seemed sly. "I just need to get these treats packaged up and we can be on our way."

Jag decided it was best to focus on the movie so he didn't stare at Ethan while he worked. Obviously, he was dealing with the side effects of inhaling too much sugar from the air, because that human shouldn't capture his attention as strongly as he had.

At least it would be over soon. Once they got through the party, Jag would be able to shed this terrible human costume and get back to his keep. He wondered idly if he'd be able to sneak some peanut butter balls back with him when it was all said and done.

Not much longer now.

Ethan gathered up the cookies, pies, and other sugary delights in plastic containers and bags, handing the pie cage to Jag to carry. When it was finally time to go, Jag felt an odd sense of anxiety at the thought of having to interact with more humans. It wasn't fear but an uncomfortable bubble of foreboding that swelled in his gut.

For a moment, he thought about demanding that he and Ethan stay inside, eat the treats themselves, and watch more odd holiday movies. That thought spurred him into action, ready to charge through this oath and get back to normal.

But Jagmarith, second son of Bolor'gath, Champion of the Blood Wars, was about to face a terror he'd never faced before.

3

SNOW & OTHER ATROCITIES

At first, Jag wasn't sure what he was seeing.

Through the open front door of Ethan's small home, a nightmare awaited them. White flakes fell from the sky like ash, coating the ground in mounds several feet high. Jag's blood ran cold in his veins, terror gripping him so tightly his muscles froze.

Snow.

"By Satan," he hissed through his teeth. "We're going to die."

Ethan, unknowing or uncaring of the danger, walked right out the door like a mad man, bundled up in a big jacket with both arms full of baked goods. Jag surged forward and wrapped his arm around Ethan's middle, pulling him back against him before he could stroll into the danger. Ethan yelped, rebalancing the goods in his arms while he leaned back into Jag, the puffy jacket a cloud between them.

"You fool! Do you not see the danger outside?!"

"W-what?" Ethan blinked up at him, his green eyes darting back outside to sweep the area. "Where?"

"Everywhere!" Jag snarled at the snow. "It will bury you alive in a flash. Frozen to the earth!"

Ethan's brows rose slowly as he turned to look at Jag. "Are ... you talking about the snow?"

"Yes!" Jag squeezed him close. "You almost walked out into it!"

"Jag, the snow is not going to bury us." Ethan laughed as he spoke. "If we stood in one place outside for a couple hours, maybe. But not instantly."

"Look how much is out there already!" Jag pointed at the mountains of snowfall.

"Yeah, dude. We're in Colorado." Ethan gave Jag's arm a reassuring pat. "It snows all the damn time, but I promise it's totally safe."

Jag growled in his chest. "I don't trust it."

"Do you trust me?"

Jag peeled his eyes from the raining storm of ice and fell into emerald pools. Inbound cold air made the tip of Ethan's nose rosy, matching the soft pink of his lips. A couple of wild curls sprouted from under the cap he wore like soft spirals of sunshine.

"Yes ..." Jag finally said, reluctantly. Ethan adjusted the things in his arms to free up one of his hands, wrapping his gloved fingers around Jag's. He gave Jag's hand a tug as he started stepping outside, waiting as Jag unglued his feet from the floor.

Even wearing the jacket Ethan had bought him, the wind still bit into Jag's skin as he stepped outside. The snow fell in waves, trickling down around them as they stepped into the storm. Jag's shoulders seized, his eyes wincing from the icy assault as he tried to look up at the sky. Flakes coated Ethan's hat and shoulders as he stood in the snow with him, a smile on his lips as he watched Jag's misery.

"Not so bad, right?" Ethan lifted his chin and opened his mouth, presenting his tongue to the sky. Jag was mesmerized as he watched the snow melt on the heat of Ethan's tongue, and he felt his phantom horns tingle again.

Thank the Winds of Hell that Ethan closed his mouth so Jag could stop staring.

"We should get going." Jag shook his hair free of flakes.

Ethan locked up his home before they made the small journey to his silver vehicle, which was parked inside of the garage. Jag was in charge of closing the door after the car was pulled outside, Ethan mentioning that the engine of the door had died some time ago. Jag nodded, but he had no idea what he was talking about.

Just like the speakers in the kitchen, the car also played the same jingles and odd songs about possessed snow creatures, grandmothers being trampled by rogue deer, and running for one's life in a sleigh through the snow. If Jag wasn't aware this holiday had roots in human religion, he would swear it was a demon-based celebration. Those all seemed like ideas his kin would come up with.

"What should I expect at this gathering?" Jag asked, watching the blur of the snow-covered surroundings pass by the car's windows.

"It's pretty relaxed," Ethan explained with a shrug. "Mostly everyone catching up and eating too much. The host of the party, Olivia, always has little gifts for everyone, so we never have to stress about buying anyone anything. Sometimes we'll break out a game and all play together." He paused and made a clicking noise with his tongue. "You know, I didn't think about this, but since you're a new face, they'll probably want to ask you to talk about yourself and ask how we met."

"That's inconvenient."

"A little bit." Ethan worried his bottom lip, his fingers tapping on the steering wheel.

"How do humans usually meet?"

"Depends, really. I met David at a party. After we talked a bit, he asked for my number and we went on a date." He shrugged, trying to pass off the story like it was a casual memory, but Jag could see the sorrow tugging at Ethan's eyes.

"That's it?" Jag scowled. "He didn't even bring you a beast's heart or the skull of a foe as an offering before he tried to court you?"

Ethan's eyes went wide as he shook his head, his gaze sliding between the road and Jag. "Uh, no. He got me flowers once."

Jag scoffed, the snort of disgust loud in the tiny car. "Flowers? What kind of spineless sack of guts and piss brings *flowers* as an offering?"

"I like flowers," Ethan argued. "I'd prefer flowers over ... heads or hearts."

Jag muttered to himself about how cowardly flowers were, but didn't press the issue. "Do we tell them we met at a party, then? Perhaps I brought you a clump of dirt to show how romantic I am."

Ethan barked a laugh. "Maybe not a party, and we'll skip the dirt. How about a coffee shop? You bought me some coffee and we bonded over our love of java."

"I would not buy you coffee as an offering of courtship." Jag snarled. "I would slay a chaos boar and bring you its tusks or wrestle a sulphur serpent to submission and rip the fangs from its skull to lay at your feet."

Ethan was silent a moment before he finally managed, "Thank you?"

"Coffee does not prove my worthiness to be yours."

"Well, maybe not in Hell, but coffee is very worthy here. Do you call where you're from Hell?"

"No, but you won't be able to pronounce it since you only have one tongue. Hell is fine for the sake of conversation. What makes coffee so precious here?"

Ethan waved his hand in the air before holding up a finger, his face a mixture of horror and curiosity as he looked toward Jag.

"Hold up. You have more than one tongue?"

"Yes."

Ethan stared, glancing back at the road to keep them from careening off the highway. "You going to explain that?"

"No."

"Rude."

"Explain the coffee, Ethan. How is it a prize?"

Ethan exhaled. "Wars have been fought over coffee. It's a very precious resource and something a lot of us cherish. Yes, it's available everywhere, but knowing what type of brew, how to have it prepared, shows attention to detail and superior taste. Very attractive indeed."

Jag was willing to allow it, since skulls, fangs, and other such *proper* things were off the table.

Flowers and coffee. How atrocious.

Jag raised an eyebrow at Ethan. "What brew did I select for you?"

"Hmmm." Ethan titled his head in thought. "Vanilla latte with a sprinkle of cinnamon on top."

"Noted." Jag felt a warm bloom in his chest, like a wasp eater flower was opening around his heart when Ethan smiled.

In only a short time, Ethan was navigating his car through a new neighborhood. The houses were a bit taller than the one Ethan lived in, the construction less weathered. Multiple vehicles lined either side of the street, so finding a place to park took longer than expected.

Jag helped grab the sweets from the car, holding the pie container with both hands as they trudged through the falling snow. Puffs of steam escaped his nose as they walked, which was almost as fascinating as the colorful lights hung all over the houses they passed. The bright glow of the twinkling colors was almost beautiful against so much white, but Jag was not a fan of the giant, inflatable monstrosities that accompanied them.

He snarled at a waving Santa that seemed trapped inside of a dome. It was not pleasant.

When they arrived at the correct home, Jag noted the lack of Santa worship. In its place was something a touch more familiar. Instead of a hideous balloon of a reindeer, Santa, or elves was a couple of skeletons wearing Santa hats posed like they were building a structure out of snow. One of the skeletons even sported a festive scarf, while another had on a Krampus sweater like Jag's.

It made him optimistic for the first time since he had dealt with the horrible snowfall.

"I like the decorations."

"Yeah, Olivia is really awesome. It's always a little bit Halloween at her place, no matter what time of year. I think you'll like her," Ethan said over his shoulder as he started up the small stairs that led to the front door. Jag went to follow but was met with resistance.

A very thin magical barrier blocked him as he tried to continue up the stairs, as if the house was encased in an invisible glass dome. He hadn't felt it walking up to the house in his human form, but he felt the sting of the weak magic once he was close enough. Jag snarled and glanced around in search of the source, trying to smell where the spell was coming from.

"Aren't you coming?" Ethan asked from the porch, his eyebrows scrunched.

"There's a barrier around the house that's preventing me from entering." Jag sniffed the air again, cursing his pathetic human nose. "It's a ward. Simple but effective against me in this weak state. This human, Olivia, is she a witch?"

"Holy shit." Ethan came back down the steps as quickly as the weather allowed. "She is, but I didn't think her witchy stuff was legit. I thought she was just really goth and liked the aesthetic or something."

"Whatever her affinity for the craft, she at least mastered the basic ward. I cannot pass."

"Wow, I will never roll my eyes at her charm gifts ever again."

Ethan swept his eyes over the porch before going to the top step and dusting something away with his boot. "Salt. She always puts salt around the house. Ok, now try."

Jag hesitantly took a careful step up, the magic still present but broken enough for him to slip through. He gave Ethan a nod and joined him for the short distance to the door. The optimism Jag had felt at seeing the holiday skeletons was melting with the presence of magic, and he only hoped the witch hadn't mastered anything beyond the simple ward. Otherwise, it was going to be a very long night.

Ethan knocked on the door, exhaling slowly with a deep puff of steam. He was nervous, Jag could tell, and he wanted to reach out and take his shoulder but the door swung open.

A woman with black and purple hair smiled brightly, wearing a sweater with a possessed snowman eating children on it.

"Ethan!" she cried in excitement, pulling the laughing Ethan into her arms for a long, happy hug. Ethan swayed within her embrace, his voice muffled in her hair as she held him. After a long pause, she released him to turn her big brown eyes Jag's way.

"Olivia, this is Jag."

"Hi, *Jag*." She slid her eyes to Ethan and gave him a very sly look. "Ethan didn't mention he was bringing a date. I dig the sweater. Come in, come in. It's fucking cold and we need to scare your date."

"Please be nice," Ethan scolded as he walked inside, stomping his boots to knock the snow free. Jag followed, mimicking his movements to try and act as human as possible.

"I'm always nice!" She batted her painted eyes, taking the containers Ethan held before calling over her shoulder. "Guys, Ethan's here with *Jag*!"

There was a mixed collection of shouted responses, mostly people yelling Ethan's name with a couple "Who's Jag?" sprinkled in. Ethan's cheeks were flushed as he hung up his coat, his green eyes moving to Jag with a trace of worry in them.

"God, I'm sorry in advance."

"I've faced worse," Jag assured him, but Ethan winced.

"I'm not sure you have."

Olivia ushered them into the kitchen where most of the guests stood around eating and drinking. A couple bodies were in the connected room on couches or chairs and gave a wave as they entered. The smells of food unfamiliar to Jag hung in the air, pleasant and inviting. A tall, black tree was tucked near the large television, covered in red lights and glittery globes that looked like eyeballs. At the very top, a silver skull was silently screaming while wearing a Santa hat.

Olivia made a show of listing off everyone's name, none of which Jag caught or would remember, but he noted that none of them were called "David." The ex that he was charged with making jealous wasn't there.

"Who else is coming tonight?" Ethan asked, obviously also noting the absence of said ex.

"Brian and Lisa will be here soon and David and Paul are coming later." Olivia passed Ethan a red cup then pointed at Jag. "What's your poison, new guy? We have all manner of adult beverages, but we also have really yummy virgin stuff if you're driving."

Jag stared since nothing the witch said made any sense. How could a drink be of a certain age or lack sexual experience? Did he even *want* a drink that could potentially have sex?

Satan below, what the hell would that even taste like?

"Jag, you like whiskey, right? Or do you want something without alcohol like a soda?" Ethan to the rescue, listing off options he at least somewhat understood.

"Whiskey." Jag nodded a thanks as Olivia passed him a cup. Human-made whiskey wasn't bad. The burn was warm and pleasant, but it didn't have the brute punch demon spirits had. It was the first mild case of homesickness to strike Jag. He wasn't ever going to get properly drunk in this realm, at least not without Sami smuggling something good in.

"So, *Jag*," Olivia sang. "What do you do for a living?"

Jag paused mid-drink. This had not been discussed previously. He most definitely could not tell a house full of humans that he was a demon warrior whose clan had plans to conquer Earth and enslave all of humanity. It would likely not go over well. With the weight of several pairs of eyes on him, Jag felt a creeping swarm of heat track up his neck and into his cheeks.

Quick, you fool. You have to say something. Anything. Make it impressive and important.

"Coffee." Jag winced. "I work with coffee."

"He's a barista." Ethan stumbled into the conversation after him. "That's actually how we met."

"Yes." Jag nodded. "That is all true and correct."

Ethan gave him a pat on his back, and Jag felt as if they had handled that situation very well. Olivia's eyebrows were raised, and someone coughed.

"O-kay," she said slowly, then lifted her drink. "Now that everyone has a drink, how about a round of Never have I Ever?" Olivia raised her voice so even the people in the adjoining room could hear. "We can kill some time while we're waiting on everyone."

Ethan leaned over to Jag and spoke softly, "It's a drinking game. If you've done the thing mentioned, you take a drink. It's easy to follow."

Jag had a follow-up question about the rules, but the game started before he had a chance to ask.

"Let's start it off super easy. Never have I ever been to my awesome winter party." She grinned over her cup as everyone took a drink. Jag followed their lead, sipping on his whiskey.

A man standing beside Olivia, whose name Jag had immediately forgotten, went next. "Never have I ever kissed a boy."

"Ew, gross," Olivia teased, not taking a drink as Jag, Ethan, and a couple of other people did. A woman beside the nameless man, whose name Jag was decently sure started with a "Th" sound, chimed in.

"Never have I ever kissed *two* boys at once!" She gave a hoot and sipped her drink, along with a few others.

And Ethan.

Jag blinked in surprise, and Ethan's cheeks flushed.

"Never have I ever," another man, perhaps Jimothy, began, "had sex in a public place."

Ethan didn't make eye contact as he took a sip of his drink to the chorus of laughter.

Interesting.

"Never have I ever …" A woman with stuffed antlers on her head spoke with a mischievous look on her face.

"Bekka, no." Ethan pointed at her.

"Run through …" she continued in a slow drawl, a wide, toothy grin across her face.

"*No.*"

"A hotel lobby …"

"It's *Christmas*," Ethan begged, but the Bekka woman did not falter and delivered the killing blow.

"Butt-ass naked with only leopard body paint on."

Ethan covered his face, sipping his drink through his fingers.

"Why a leopard?" Was the only thing Jag could think to ask.

"Why *were* you a leopard, Ethan?" Olivia tilted her head, her smile so wide it made her cheeks pink.

"You're such a bitch." Ethan shut his eyes. After a long sigh, he added in a mumble, "Because I was on the prowl for man meat."

The kitchen burst into laughter, and Ethan yelled over their chorus, "It was a dare and I was really drunk!"

"I think Jag is learning some stuff about you," Olivia chided playfully.

"I certainly am." Jag watched Ethan's neck become splotchy,

both hands covering his face. This sweet little human who baked cookies and liked sweaters was a little wilder than Jag had realized.

He felt a very strange mix of conflicting emotions, seeing Ethan burning with embarrassment beside him. Jag was torn between the desire to tuck Ethan into his side and protect him and to demand more information about other naked exploits. What did Ethan look like as a leopard? What did he look like as a *naked* leopard?

What sort of *man meat* did he prowl for?

"Your turn, Jag," the woman beside him pulled him from his thoughts. "I think Ethan deserves to learn a little bit about *you*, don't you think?"

Having a sudden audience was a little unnerving, even for an experienced demon warrior. They were clearly expecting something grand and embarrassing, or at least insightful. But Jag was a demon from the burning landscape of their nightmares. He certainly didn't have common stories.

Ethan's emerald eyes sparkled as they looked up at him, his cheeks rosy from smiling and hiding behind his fingers. How could he still look so sweet after admitting to prowling for sex as a naked leopard?

Humans were tricky creatures.

And Jag couldn't let him down.

"Never have I ever," Jag summoned courage with a deep breath, "gotten a succubus's horn stuck in a sensitive area during an orgy."

There was a lot of silence, staring, and only one other person took a drink.

"It wasn't a horn, but it was a dildo, so I'm counting it," the woman said with a shrug.

Jag liked that human.

"That's a lot to unpack," Ethan said slowly, his eyes wide. "I have so many questions."

"I think we all have so many questions," Olivia added with a laugh. "But we'll circle back. Parth, your turn."

"How the fuck do I follow that?" the man beside Jag yelled.

Ethan tugged on Jag's sleeve, leaning in closer to whisper. His warm breath smelled like alcohol and something fruit across Jag's cheek, and it was almost as intoxicating as the whiskey Jag was sipping. "Can you tell me more about that?"

Jag felt his horns itch, a small tug where they should be.

"Maybe later." He set his drink down. "Where is the restroom?"

Ethan pointed around the corner. "Down the hall, second door on the left. Hey, I'm not going to forget that story."

Jag smirked and made his escape, slipping away from the game to find the proper place to relieve himself.

It would prove to be more harrowing than expected.

As Jag tried to enter the bathroom, he was met with a blinding spear of pain through his temples. It was as if a sharp rock was driving itself between his skull and brain and twisting, grinding gritty pebbles behind his eyes. With a hiss he jerked away from the bathroom door, the pain fading the moment he cleared the doorframe.

Jag rubbed his face with his palm, easing the last bit of the sting from his head as he scanned the area. There was no salt like before, no barrier in place to keep him from entering. He leaned toward the doorway again, feeling the threat of the jagged pain press against his temple as soon as he was near it.

Whatever was causing this pain, it was inside the bathroom.

Fucking great.

The pressure in his bladder wasn't unbearable, but it was present. It wasn't something he could ignore forever.

Jag peered into the bathroom, staying an arm's length away to keep the pain at bay. The small room was unassuming enough, with black- and white-striped wallpaper, skulls painted across a plastic shower curtain, and matching rugs, soap dispenser, and so on. There was absolutely nothing worth noting until his eyes landed on a small bowl above the toilet. Beside the small vials of spray to mask the scent of defecation, a tiny wicker bowl of minerals caught the dim glow of a skull-shaped light sticking out of a socket.

Jag didn't recognize most of them, but he did see the pyrite.

Its shiny, dark surface mocked him.

Simple but effective. Just like the damn salt.

Jag rubbed his eyes again, ignored his bladder, and walked back to the kitchen. It was going to be a very long night.

If it wasn't optimal that he impressed people at this party, Jag would have relieved himself in the hallway to prove a point. But if he had any wish to return home, he knew he had to pretend to be a well-mannered human for a bit longer.

When Jag returned to the group, he scanned the people present to see if any new additions had arrived. No one new caught his attention, and he felt annoyance flare in his chest.

"Hey." Ethan handed him a full cup of liquid Jag couldn't ingest since his bladder was already full. "You having a good time?"

"When is David supposed to arrive?" Jag kept his voice low. "I don't like being in this form."

"I think soon. Are you okay?" Worry creased Ethan's face, which caused a very unwelcome feeling of guilt to swell in Jag. Jag was already feeling weak and helpless in this wormy form; now he was feeling guilty for making Ethan upset. He wanted to be angry, to demand that Ethan do something to free him from his human confines.

But the anger wouldn't come. It was trapped below a heavy stone of guilt that pulsed with the need to comfort. He wanted to see Ethan smile more than he wanted to have horns again.

And for the first time in Jagmarith's centuries-long life, he felt a little afraid.

"Ethan ... I ..." Jag stammered, tripping over his words as

he tried to wrangle what it was he was feeling. Had this small, sweet little human cast a spell on him? Was this part of the oath? Did his human form have a fatal emotional problem?

Emerald eyes bored into Jag's black soul and reflected back something beautiful. The babble of voices around them dropped away, and all there was for eternity was Ethan of Clan Montgomery.

"Yeah, Jag?" Ethan whispered, the soft sound carrying the weight of it all. How lovely his name sounded on Ethan's lips.

Jag opened his mouth to speak, but his human form betrayed him again.

Pressure seized his nasal cavities, locking his chest into a sharp inhale. Without warning, the pressure released, and a shotgun blast of spit and phlegm flew directly into Ethan's face.

But oh, it didn't stop there.

Jag continued to sneeze in an uncontrollable spasm, his eyes watering to the point of total blindness. His nose oozed, his lungs burned from constant coughing and sneezing, and the skin across his face burned red hot.

The constant barrage of violent reactions made the pressure in his bladder worse, and for a horrifying moment, Jag was worried he'd piss himself in the kitchen.

Unable to demand answers, Jag simply screamed in agony and covered his face with his arm.

"Oh my God!" Ethan wailed, trying to steady Jag. "Are you having a reaction to something?"

Jag choked, gulping down some air to try and speak. This sparked another round of hiccupping coughs that sent his sneezing into overdrive. A bitter bile coated the back of his tongue, the taste sharp and pungent as it seeped down the back of his throat.

"S-sage!" Jag managed through a strangled throat. "F-fucking *sage!*"

"Is he allergic?" Olivia shrieked from somewhere nearby. "I'm so sorry!"

Jag tried to scream at her for the audacity of her actions but was crippled by a wave of coughs that punched him in the bladder. The world around him was a watery blur, which created further obstacles when he tried to make his escape. Someone was tugging his arm, steering him blindly through the house as Jag tried to get his mucus under control.

"Why would you burn sage right now?" Ethan was scolding Olivia, speaking from Jag's side.

"I-I was just showing off my new smudge stick! I'm so, *so* sorry! Wash his face with some water, that'll help."

Through the tears, Jag could make out a door frame, and he prayed to Satan it was the way out of the house. Fresh air would be the only relief from the madness.

The grinding pain of a rock shard to his temple was a clue to which door it was. Jag jerked backward, the new barrage of pain to his sensitive, dripping body making him howl in agony.

He was beyond painfully aware he was a demon inside a witch's house. How had things gone so very wrong while staring into the eyes of someone so beautiful?

Was this payback for the centuries of war and bloodshed? Had fate turned against him after he had pledged his life to his clan, battling endless onslaughts of fellow demons over the right to rule over the humans? In those moments, Jag was starting to believe he had somehow personally upset Satan and was dying a slow death of embarrassment and snot.

"Outside, outside!!" Jag yelled through his hands.

"Okay, okay!" Ethan tugged him away from the door, yelping an apology as he let Jag's shoulder crash into the wall.

They passed blurry bodies as they ran through the house in a mad dash for the front door. The sudden blast of cold was as wonderful as it was horrifying, and Jag couldn't decide which reaction he felt the strongest. Fresh, biting air ripped at his wet face as he inhaled deeply, trying to flush the burning sage from his body.

Ethan eased him down onto the steps, brushing away the strands of hair that stuck to Jag's face. Olivia was hovering nearby, begging for her apology to be accepted as she offered remedies. Jag wanted to turn her inside out and pose her corpse next to her holiday skeletons, but instead he hung his head in pain.

"Can you get us some water?" Ethan asked Olivia, sending her back inside.

Without her panicked squawking, it was peaceful but terribly cold. Gentle fingers touched under Jag's chin, lifting it gently as a warm, wet cloth started dabbing his face.

"I'm so sorry, Jag." Ethan swiped away the gross substances leaking from Jag's face. "I should have been paying attention."

Jag tried to speak, but his throat was raw and everything burned. Instead, a pathetic whimper bubbled up from his chest, and he hated how sad it sounded.

Satan help him, if his clan found out about this, he was fairly sure he'd be banished.

"This was such a stupid idea," Ethan continued, his voice heavy with sorrow. "You're hurt because I made you come here tonight."

"I'm not hurt." Jag's voice was hoarse but he still got the words out. "I've faced much worse than a witch's smudge stick, Ethan. I do not need your pity."

"I don't pity you, Jag. I'm just sorry that I put you in a bad situation. I was really having fun with you today, and I feel like this ruined it." He ran the cloth over both of Jag's eyes gently, and the burning sensation began to fade.

Carefully, Jag cracked open his eyes and blinked away the tears.

"I fear I won't be impressing anyone now," Jag admitted, sniffling away the lingering threat of another sneeze. Ethan let a small smile grace his lips.

"I dunno. After we get you cleaned up, you'll be okay."

"I feel like all the liquid from my head has escaped out of my nose."

"Yeah, you do kind of look like someone maced you." Ethan brushed the washcloth over his nose again, glancing up as Olivia returned with some water.

"I have all the windows open to try and get the sage out of the house," she said, wringing her hands together. "But I don't know if it's a great idea to come back in. Maybe you both should head home so he can rest. I'll pack up some food for you—"

"No!" Jag and Ethan both erupted at the same time, making Olivia jump.

"I just ... wanted to make sure I saw everyone," Ethan said, recovering.

"I'm feeling much bet—" the sneeze that had been threatening Jag chose that moment to surge forward, fooling no one.

"I'll make sure Brian and Lisa know you send your love. Plus, you dodged a bullet anyway. David just called and said he can't make it. At least you don't have to deal with that drama tonight." Olivia turned on her heels and said over her shoulder, "Let me pack up some food and get your presents."

"H-he's not coming?" Ethan stood up, almost slipping on the icy steps.

"Thank God, right?" Olivia disappeared back inside the house, leaving Ethan standing there looking horrified.

It had all been for nothing.

The embarrassment, the horrible sneezing fit, being forced to pretend to be human – all of it.

For nothing.

"Oh no," he whispered, but it was lost in the fury boiling in Jag's ears. "Jag, I—"

"How in hell am I supposed to fulfil this fucking oath now?"

Jag snapped, his head pounding from inhaling toxic sage. "All of this nonsense and torture was for *nothing!*"

"Jag, I'm sorry! I'll figure it out!" Ethan gripped the railing, leaning out of Jag's way as he lurched to his feet.

"I have been torn from my home, forced to be in this *pathetic* form, had to put up with your idiotic customs." Jag plucked at his sweater then pointed towards the house. "Been exposed to magic, which I *loathe*, and then chased out of a house with sage! All because *you* cannot get over being heartbroken by a man who brought you *flowers!* Pathetic!"

Ethan's jaw tightened, his eyes gluing themselves to the ground. Jag felt the pinpricks of guilt starting to form, causing his anger to consume him. Jag stormed off, needing to put some distance between himself and the source of his conflicting emotions, so he could properly stew.

The snow had stopped falling, but it was still very cold outside. Jag's anger kept him warm as he walked, aiming for nowhere in particular, letting his fires burn. It was only then he remembered how badly he had to relieve himself, so he decided to do so on one of the inflatable Santas in someone's yard.

It helped him feel a little better.

"Sami!" Jag called once he was done, folding his arms over his chest. A ripple in the air wiggled into existence and Sami climbed free.

"Yes, Master? Oh—!" Sami's eyes widened, his ears perking straight up like a cat's. "Is this *snow*, Master?! How exciting!"

"You're not terrified of it?" Jag scowled as Sami scooped up some snow in his bare hands, formed it into a ball, and threw it at a wooden reindeer. The little familiar's laugh was a whip crack through the quiet street.

"What do you need, Master? Did you fulfil the oath?"

"No. The ex isn't coming." Jag huffed out steam from his lips.

"Oh, that's disappointing."

"Yes." Jag rubbed at his chest, a stabbing ache starting to settle into his bones.

Sami watched him, his ears swiveling. "Ethan is a very nice human, wouldn't you say?"

Jag didn't answer because he wasn't sure what to say. Ethan was very nice. He was handsome and cooked delicious food. His smile was as bright as the midday sun and warm like the lakes of fire back home. Clearly he was wild, as the leopard-paint story proved, and Jag was aware that he still had so much to learn about the man.

The same man who had just cleaned off his face when he was dripping and disgusting.

"A demon doesn't have room for *nice* in his life, Sami. I'm a Hell warrior charged with fighting for the right to rule over the human realm. What in Satan's name would I do with *nice?*"

Sami did this little musical hum he did when he was thinking. "I would say that a Hell warrior charged with fighting to rule over the human realm would have nothing to prove to anyone but himself. Especially those who wear his clan's armor and have victories coated in the blood of his enemies. Why, I would wager that a demon like that could have whatever he wanted in his life. Even if it is nice."

Jag inhaled slowly, the ache in his chest flexing into something entirely different.

He had fucked up.

Royally.

He had called Ethan pathetic and raised his voice to him. Jag had made him feel small. And alone.

That would not do.

"Sami, I need you to get me some things."

4

A PROPER PROPOSAL

Ethan was waiting by the steps when Jag returned to Olivia's house. He was holding Jag's coat and a couple of bags. The cheer around his eyes was gone, even if he did wear a smile for the sake of saving face.

It hurt Jag to know that false smile was because of him. It hurt even more when Ethan didn't look him in the eyes when he handed him his coat.

Olivia wished them both a good night, and the walk back to Ethan's car was very quiet. Jag felt compelled to say something to break the tension, but nothing in his head sounded quite right. Being a demon and a warrior, apologizing wasn't something he had done, for anyone, ever. There was no such custom back home, so Jag wasn't familiar with the language needed to express his sense of shame for being a jackass.

He'd only hoped what he had planned would be enough.

There was also the very real possibility that his demon heritage and very limited understanding of human culture would backfire tremendously. Doubt was a foul thing, like a weighted sludge that one cannot shake off, and it clung to Jag for dear life.

He cleared his throat carefully as they got into the car. "Ethan."

"Can we not?" Ethan cranked his car to life, refusing to look his direction. It hurt.

"I wanted to discuss ..."

"Please?" The waver in Ethan's voice threatened tears, and Jag locked his jaw into place. If he caused Ethan to shed tears, he'd never forgive himself. The car was silent as they drove. No music on the radio, no banter filling the quiet. Only the hum of the engine, the dull swish of a passing car.

Nerves danced through Jag's gut like a thousand little beetles, causing him to fidget quietly in his seat. Somehow the car ride seemed like an eternity, a much worse torture than the sage and pyrite combined.

Ethan still refused to speak to or look at him as they arrived back home. He didn't even ask Jag to get the garage door, only climbed out into the cold and handled it himself. Jag felt horrible for not offering in time and was helpless as Ethan gathered all the bags alone as well.

Jag's heart was hammering against his ribs as they went inside, and for a brief moment he thought Ethan would disappear upstairs without going to the kitchen. But after dropping some bags off in the living room, he silently shuffled into the kitchen to put the food away, flicking on the light as he did.

A terrified scream burst from Ethan and he dropped the bags, scrambling backward against the counters with wide eyes. It was not the reaction Jag had hoped for when he arranged for the surprise. Sitting on the dining table in a crystal vase filled with acid was the hydra lilies Jag had asked Sami to bring. The familiar had done a fantastic job with the color arrangement.

Each lily head hissed and danced like a serpent, their petals lined with dagger teeth that sparkled in the light. The beautiful display of colors was as vibrant and diverse as the cookies they had decorated earlier that day.

"W-what the hell is that?" Ethan panted, pointing at the vase from across the kitchen.

"Hydra lilies." Jag played with the hem of his sweater. "You don't like them?"

"*Hydra* lilies?" Ethan swung his head from Jag to the lilies, then back to Jag. "Why would you bring monsters into the house?"

"They're flowers," Jag explained, his confidence starting to wane.

Ethan stared at Jag, the look of horror sliding into confusion as he glanced back at the vase. "They are?" Jag nodded and Ethan swallowed. "Are they ... safe?"

"Oh Satan, no. Their bite is acidic."

"Then *why are they here?*" Ethan's confusion was hardening into anger, the sound a dagger in Jag's heart.

"Because I'm a fool," Jag said quickly. "I cannot wrangle my emotions around you, Ethan. You confuse me. Everything logical is telling me that what I'm feeling shouldn't be happening, and I've been fighting with it since the moment I saw you."

Jag took a long breath and moved so he could stand before Ethan. Thankfully, Ethan was stunned into silence, so Jag could continue.

"What I said earlier was ... shameful. And I regret my words. The lilies are to show you how I truly feel and are also my offering to you."

"Offering?" Ethan whispered, emerald eyes jumping as he watched Jag's face. "Offering for what?"

Jag inhaled and puffed out his chest. "To be yours."

"Are ..." Ethan swallowed. "Are you asking me out?"

Jag squinted. "Out where?"

"No, I mean ..." Ethan shook his head. "Are you asking to be with me? Romantically?"

Jag reached up and cupped Ethan's jaw. His cheek was warm and rosy under Jag's thumb. "If you'll have me, Ethan."

Ethan exhaled in a rush, his fingers curling into Jag's Krampus sweater. He stood on his toes and groaned. "God, why are you so tall? I can't kiss you dramatically from down here!"

Jag leaned down the rest of the way so they could kiss dramatically, and Jag was not prepared for the sensation. Ethan's lips were rose-petal soft but deliciously forceful, capturing Jag's mouth just right. Teeth nipped at Jag's bottom lip; a hot tongue lapped and tangled with his like a twisting vine. The bite of alcohol still lingered in Ethan's mouth, the fruity mix with a hint of something sweet making Jag starve to taste every inch of him.

The tingling where his horns should be seemed much stronger now.

Ethan eased back far enough to catch his breath, his grip still tight in Jag's sweater. "Let's go upstairs. I can reach you if you're lying down."

Ethan yelped as Jag picked him up and tossed him over his shoulder, Ethan's body bouncing as he laughed.

"You're a damn caveman!" Ethan yelled, his feet playfully kicking as Jag held onto his thighs.

"I'm a demon." Jag took two steps at a time, sprinting up the stairs to drop Ethan onto the mattress. "And I like sex."

Ethan bounced on the mattress and bit his bottom lip as he aimed his emerald eyes up at Jag. He pressed back into the blankets as Jag crawled over him, squeezing his thighs around Jag's hips. Their mouths clashed again, soft moans escaping Ethan as Jag rolled his hips. There was far too much fabric between them, so Jag reached back over his head and peeled off his sweater, tossing it aside.

Ethan did the same, and for the first time Jag could see that the red from his cheeks and neck bled slightly onto his milky chest as well. A wave of lust pulsed through Jag, his horns pressing against the fleshy cage of his human form so sharply that it made him hiss.

"Jag," Ethan breathed, his curls wild against the pillow. "I want you to fuck me."

That did not help the horn situation. Jag growled and massaged his forehead, trying to will the damn things back down. Ethan sat up on his knees and slipped his fingers behind Jag's neck, his other hand sliding down Jag's chest. Jag wondered idly if Ethan could feel how hard his heart was pounding.

"Keep the bed warm for me?" Ethan smiled. "Give me a couple minutes."

Jag tried to drag him back down onto the mattress, but Ethan slipped free with a cheeky grin and disappeared into the bathroom. Jag pressed both of his palms against his forehead, massaging the pulses from his other form. His horns tingled and stung, like the tips were just barely under the surface.

"Control yourself, Jagmarith." Jag took a long breath. "You're the master of your form; your lust is not."

While Ethan was in the bathroom, Jag finished disrobing and climbed back onto the bed. He was ready to pounce on Ethan as soon as he came back, and the anticipation was curling his toes. It was also giving him time to reign in the electric buzz under his skin and keep the excitement from getting the better of him.

"You're in control," he whispered again. "Don't embarrass yourself."

The bathroom door opened, and Ethan emerged, gloriously naked.

His skin was pink and flushed, sunlight curls wild, emerald eyes hooded and dark with want. His excitement was evident, standing tall, and the slow stroke he gave himself lit Jag's fuse.

"Satan help me," Jag whispered as a wicked vibration ran up his spine. Ethan crawled over the bed toward him like a hungry cat, sitting up only to swing one knee over Jag's thighs. He smelled like woodsy soap and citrus, and Jag was drunk on how warm his skin was.

Through the centuries, Jagmarith, second son of Bolor'gath,

Champion of the Blood Wars, had been known for his strict discipline and steely nerves. He had killed many, bedded even more and was well versed in the arts of pleasure, hedonism, and eroticism. Incubi fed on his lust for days, demons quaked under his touch, and he'd even had a wild fling with a Jorogumo in his youth.

But seeing this human straddling his lap, green eyes blown wide with lust, lips kissed pink and wet, broke him.

Jag's horns bursts through his skin, swelling and curling back into their natural position. His body expanded, skin rushing back to its natural crimson color as his muscles and bones stretched back into position. Behind him, a long tail with a blunt spade at the tip uncurled from his spine and slid across the blanket like a red snake.

As Jag shifted into his demon form, Ethan threw both hands over his mouth in alarm and fell backward.

"I swear that's never happened to me before," Jag said quickly, just as his pendant shattered into dust across his chest.

"Holy shit." Ethan pushed himself up onto his elbows. "Do you have a tail? Did you have one before?"

"No, I only grow that when I'm turned on." Jag rubbed the back of his neck. "I can call Sami for another pendant. Maybe if I just keep my eyes shut I can stay a human …"

"Are you fucking kidding?" Ethan shook his head, his curls bouncing. "Jag, you're … *so* hot like this."

Jag blinked. "I didn't want to scare you."

Ethan crawled back over him, sitting on his lap and pressing his rigid cock against Jag's. "Do I feel scared?"

"Ethan," Jag growled, his eyes rolling back. "I don't know if you can handle me like this."

Teeth nipped at Jag's earlobe, warm breath curling into the shell as Ethan spoke. "Fuck me, Jagmarith."

Ethan landed on his back as Jag flipped him backward and blanketed him with his mighty form. Ethan whimpered soft moans of delight as Jag tasted him, roaming his tongues and teeth over Ethan's neck and chest. Jag was mindful of his teeth, some much pointier and more dangerous to sweet human skin, as he lapped and nibbled. The flush of pink over Ethan was delicious, warm, and succulent all the way down his belly.

Pearls of lust were beading at Ethan's head, begging to be tasted, and Jag flexed his jaw and tongues.

"If it gets to be too much," Jag said, meeting Ethan's eyes as he lifted his head. "Tell me to stop, and I will."

"'Kay," Ethan panted, his fingers digging into the blankets as he ran his teeth over his lip again. He was beautiful, like a plump peach made to bite and savor. As he opened his jaw, Jag wondered if Ethan would taste just as juicy. Both of his tongues slithered forward, long and thick like wet tentacles sliding over Ethan's skin.

Ethan gasped, his knuckles flexing as his eyes grew wide. Jag watched his face for signs of fear as he carefully moved his tongues over the soft skin of Ethan's inner thighs, testing and teasing. After a couple breaths, Ethan leaned his head back and shut his eyes, his fingers relaxing.

"Feels good," he whispered, opening his eyes again. "Can I grab your horns?"

Jag nodded since his tongues were occupied, his eyes fluttering shut the moment Ethan's fingers gripped his horns. The bony objects protruding out of Jag's head had no nerve endings, but just knowing Ethan was gripping them while he devoured him sent a bolt of lust straight to his cock.

Jag slithered one of his tongues over to Ethan's cock, circling his balls slowly before running it up to the tip. The bite of flavor from the pearly liquid made Jag growl, and Ethan hissed through his teeth. Much, much better than a peach. Ethan tasted like sex and desire; he was a forbidden fruit Jag had never dreamed of consuming.

Which made him all the more delicious.

Jag slipped his tail around Ethan's waist as he curled one of his tongues over Ethan's cock, stroking and squeezing with the wet muscle. The other tongue slipped down further, giving a testing lap across Ethan's entrance.

Jag's tail held Ethan still as he arched his back, his fingers gripping Jag's horns tight.

"Oh my God, that feels so good." Ethan exhaled quickly. "I've never had a blow job and that at the same time. That's really intense."

Good.

Jag wanted Ethan to feel pleasures like no mere mortal human could give him. The thought of seeing Ethan ruined by a mind-altering orgasm made Jag's cock jerk in anticipation.

His second tongue swirled and teased while the first one gripped and licked. Ethan writhed, hissing and groaning as Jag's tongues paid him wonderful, tortuous attention. Jag's sharp fingers traced lightly over the soft flesh of Ethan's thighs and belly, occasionally pressing into the meat of his backside to give an extra bite to the barrage of pleasure.

Jag could feel Ethan's cock swell and grow iron hard, his stomach clenching as he pushed on the mattress with his feet.

"Stop," Ethan whimpered. "Stop, stop."

Jag loosened his tail and retracted his tongues. "Too much?"

"If you had kept going, I was going to come. I want you to fuck me before that." Ethan's gaze dropped to the well-endowed pride between Jag's legs, the attention making the appendage perk up even more. Sitting up, Ethan reached into the drawer beside the bed and handed Jag a plastic bottle with a snapped lid.

Jag gave the thing a puzzled look and Ethan winked.

"Lube. Humans need extra help fitting big things into tight spaces."

Jag shivered at the promise, and Ethan grinned.

"How do you want me?"

Jag could barely contain the volume of his voice as he spoke. "All fours."

Ethan slipped onto his stomach, the move relaxed and languid as he propped himself onto his knees and spread them apart. Jag squeezed the flesh of his backside with both hands, pressing the underside of his cock against Ethan's entrance as a hint of what was to come. Ethan purred into the mattress, stretching out before peeking back over his shoulder.

Such a wild, sweet thing that Jag was about to send spiraling over the edge.

The liquid in the bottle was thick and slippery, and Jag made sure to be generous with his application. He wanted Ethan begging for release, not aching from lack of attention to his needs. When he was properly coated and Ethan was pouting for attention, he slipped his tail around Ethan's waist again.

Ethan gave a happy bark as Jag gave his ass a slap, lining himself up and holding Ethan still. He thought about distracting him with his tongues, but he wanted Ethan to feel every inch as he buried himself inside of him.

Jag eased himself in, holding Ethan steady as his muscles clenched and relaxed. Ethan grunted and groaned, his hands tangling in the sheets as the demon worked his massive cock into his body. The union was an unholy abomination to the sensibilities of both sides, and for some reason that turned Jag on even more. A demon fucking a human. It was so taboo. So sinful.

It made his horns feel like they were burning, like his bones had become glowing embers under his skin.

Ethan gave a happy sob as he was finally impaled, Jag buried to the root inside the sweet peach in front of him. Jag was careful of his claws as he wrapped his hands around Ethan's waist, sliding back to watch himself push back inside. Ethan groaned for more, his emerald eyes shining from a mess of wild curls.

Oh, Jag would give him more. So, so much more.

Jag opened his jaw and let his tongues slither out again,

reaching under Ethan to lick and tease his cock as he snapped his hips forward. Jag could taste the lovely, bitter bite of Ethan's pre-cum, the taste even more intoxicating when combined with the sounds of pounding flesh and moaning. Ethan was babbling nonsense as Jag fucked him, the tight pressure of his body squeezing Jag for all it was worth.

Heat and fire churned in Jag's bones, fireflies swarmed in his belly as pressure curled at the base of his spine. All of his senses were lost in Ethan, his woodsy smell, the bite of his taste, the symphony of pleasure singing from his lips. It was as close to heaven as a demon could reach.

Ethan panted and pleaded, his warning drowned out as he screamed Jagmarith's name. A blast of flavor coated Jag's tongue, pulses dripping over his tastebuds as he continued to squeeze. Jag felt his horns burst into flames, the coil inside of him snapping as his orgasm raced to the surface. The rush of ecstasy made him roar, the sound twisted and powerful.

Ethan gave a long groan, his eyes rolling back into his head as more of his flavor spilled out over Jag's tongue, a fresh orgasm rocking his body at the feeling of a demon coming inside of him.

Jag's bones began to cool, the fire raging over his horns died down to embers, and he carefully freed himself from the panting and spent Ethan.

The sheets were beyond salvaging. And Jag wasn't sure how to tell Ethan he had burned his ceiling. He decided he'd tell him later.

Instead, Jag cleaned up the mildly comatose, post-orgasm Ethan, wrapping him in a clean blanket and stripping the dirty sheets from the bed. Ethan didn't seem to care that he was swaddled and tucked against Jag's chest; the pure bliss on his face made Jag's chest light.

"You're so warm," Ethan said idly. "Like a heated blanket."

Jag hummed, breathing in the citrus smell of his curls.

"Hey, Jag?" Ethan lifted his chin. "We didn't use a condom. Are there like ... STDs in hell?"

"Nothing I can give to you. Unless you're part spider."

"Spider? Jesus, Jag." Ethan chuckled. "I don't want to know."

"It was a long time ago and I was young."

Ethan wiggled one arm free to give Jag's chest a pat. "We've all been there."

They lay together in bliss for a while, enjoying the silence and comfort of each other's arms. It was Ethan who finally spoke, bringing up the topic they had been avoiding.

"What are we going to do about the oath?"

Jag took a deep breath. "I don't know."

"Well." He blinked up at Jag again, his eyes still as brilliant and lovely as ever. "We usually have a New Year's party. That's in about a week. We can try again then."

Jag thought about it, then tilted his head in thought. "What about after that?"

"After New Year's?" Ethan shrugged and dared to smile. "Maybe Valentine's Day. That's in a couple months."

"Maybe after that." Jag pressed his lips to Ethan's curls. "There are plenty of holidays to try."

ETHAN & JAG DESTROY THE WORLD

5

THE DEVIL'S HOLIDAY

Jagmarith, second son of Bolor'gath, Champion of the Blood Wars and carrier of his clan's armor, had been living with a human for nine months.

During that time, Jag had learned much about the human world and its odd cultural traditions. As if the winter months weren't bad enough with their strange holidays, deadly snow and abundance of sugar-infused confections—but humans seemed to find a reason to celebrate even the most mundane things—come the spring, Jag was offended by the misconception of what a human heart looked like. In every location Ethan took him to, misshapen representations of hearts hung all around, normally surrounded by naked, winged children with weapons. The idea of displaying hearts to declare one's affection sounded correct, especially if those hearts were of rival lovers or great beasts. But Ethan was horrified by that notion.

Apparently the glittery, ass-shaped hearts were supposed to be accompanied with candy and flowers.

Flowers.

Jag hated flowers.

His last attempt at securing worthy flowers for Ethan had

marvelous outcomes when it came to the bedroom, but the next morning was a different story. Half of Ethan's table had been consumed, and one of the flowers spit acid on a painting of a horse. Sami had to take them back, and new furniture had to be obtained.

Instead of opting for gifts Jag was accustomed to, he tried to be more traditional in the human sense and bought Ethan some candy (with Sami's help). It was on Valentine's Day that Jag learned Ethan was allergic to coconut, and they spent the afternoon in the hospital.

It was not ideal.

The next holiday after stupid Valentine's Day was a celebration of clovers and alcohol. Jag liked that one. Human alcohol was decent, and in great quantities, Jag could even get a little drunk in his human form. Ethan taught him the ways of karaoke and introduced him to the wonders of the root vegetable: the potato.

The summer had a holiday celebrating Ethan's country's independence from a king, which included explosions, more alcohol, great quantities of grilled meat, and outdoor activities. The story of the bloody victory of the Americans wasn't as grand as Jag was hoping for. There were no champions in the sense he was used to, no creative ways to display the mangled bodies of the fallen, and the battle cry was a poem.

They didn't even go back to the king and skin him alive. What kind of victory didn't have flaying?

Ethan had assured Jag that within human history there were plenty of stories that had these elements, but they weren't tied to the holiday.

Human holidays, Jag had decided, were mostly an excuse to eat and drink and forget about life for a while. It wasn't grand or a testament to their might or fighting abilities like the festivities back home. But it was nice. Mainly because Ethan liked them.

And Jag liked Ethan.

Each time one of the parties Jag was dragged to began to get under his skin, from the misshapen hearts to the bland history lessons with not near enough spine displays mentioned, Ethan would smile and take Jag's hand in his.

Everything seemed to fall away after that. Jag didn't want to be anywhere else in the human world or his own.

Jag was reflecting on how deeply the sweet human had buried himself into his properly shaped heart as Ethan scrolled through his phone, chatting about pumpkins. When his hazel eyes lifted from the screen and blinked at Jag, he realized Ethan was waiting for an answer to a question Jag didn't catch.

"Do you have something like this where you're from?"

"Hm?" Jag glanced towards the small illuminated screen to see the smattering of images that made no sense to him. A gourd was hollowed out and had a grinning face carved into it. Children were standing in mockeries of phantoms and ghouls, carrying buckets filled with candy. A woman and a man were posing as a hotdog and a condiment.

"Why would we dress as food and mutilate gourds?"

"That's just what we do. Well, that's what people in America do." Ethan shrugged. Jag lifted his arm as Ethan leaned into him, a move that had become as normal as taking a breath. "We also dress up as monsters, ghosts, ghouls, and demons. I mean, it is the 'Devil's Holiday' after all."

This surprised Jag. "You mean Hallow's Eve?"

"We call it Halloween." Ethan nodded. "You have that back home?"

"Of course. It's sacred." Jag once again peered at the digital screen as Ethan scrolled through homes decorated like cemeteries with stringy cotton spread over the foam headboards. "Explain."

"We sort of celebrate the macabre and the scary to help us feel less scared by death and the unknown. There's candy, costumes, decorations...it's really fun. It was always my dad's favorite holiday. He would make the house look ghastly, with fog machines and these big, cheesy robotic statues that moved around and scared kids." Ethan's smile didn't quite reach his eyes. "I miss that."

Jag didn't understand what a fog machine was or robots with cheese in them, but he could tell those things were important to Ethan.

"Tell me more."

"I typically always wanted to be a Power Ranger—"

"What is a Power Ranger?"

Ethan scoffed. "They're the defenders of Earth, Jag. I can't believe I've failed you by not showing you Earth's mightiest heroes." He flicked his thumbs across the screen, summoning images of warriors in brightly colored, tight-fitting, cloth outfits. There was no armor to be seen, only helmets, boots, and gloves.

Jag refrained from commenting, allowing Ethan to continue. "I would watch this show every day when I was a kid. My favorite Halloween, I got to go as the Blue Ranger, and Mom got me the gloves that made the swishing noises from the show. I was *the coolest* kid." He let out a laugh, his cheeks getting rosy. "I actually had the biggest crush on the Green Ranger, but don't tell anyone."

It was obvious that these small, acrobatic warriors meant a lot to Ethan. While it seemed impossible that the puny humans in bright colors could have saved the realm from anything, Jag could see that Ethan admired them.

"Dad would be a big werewolf or something with a scary mask. Mom was a witch because she needed something easy to put on before running around with me and my friends." Ethan scrolled further down to a picture of children holding out their buckets of candy. "We'd go door to door asking for candy, which is what they're doing here."

"Trick or treat?" Jag hummed. "You demand candy under threat of mischief?"

"Something like that."

Jag nodded approvingly.

Ethan continued. "We'd stay out all night, come home hyper on sugar, eat too much candy, and pass out. It was kind of the one night a year we could be unapologetically kids and enjoy living in a fantasy for a while. Dad made it extra special with decorating the house."

"You don't decorate like you do for Christmas?" Jag was surprised when Ethan hesitated.

"No. I don't have kids so..." He trailed off, shrugging. "I dunno. What do you do for Hallow's Eve?"

The change in subject was not lost on Jag. "Not this." He smirked when Ethan chuckled. "We don't celebrate holidays the same as humans."

"What do you do?" Ethan flicked through the pictures, much less enthusiastically than before.

"Our holidays are either battles or orgies."

Ethan blinked, staring a moment. "That's it?"

"Yes."

"It's either one or the other?"

"Sometimes both." Jag was confused when Ethan laughed. "Those are my favorites."

"Demons." Ethan sighed. "Which is Hallow's Eve?"

"Both." Jag shrugged. "With a feast."

"Wow, that's...a lot of things happening."

"Yes." Jag curled his arm around Ethan protectively. "Ethan. We should decorate for Halloween."

"What?" His laugh was halfhearted and deflated. "Nah. We'll just be going to Olivia's party anyway. We don't need to do that."

"You told me during the winter that holidays were important to your clan. Traditions are meant to be honored."

Ethan rotated beside Jag, sitting up straight to look at Jag properly. "Really?"

"Yes. We will make the proper preparations as we did for

Christmas. I feel more confident about my abilities to assist in this theme than any other so far." Jag gave a nod. "We will turn your home into a nightmare that will haunt children until their dying days."

A mixture of amused terror rippled over his handsome features. "Maybe not that strong, but I get what you mean. Thanks, Jag."

Jag mirrored Ethan's sunbeam smile, accepting the kiss Ethan planted against his lips. As they settled back into bed together, Ethan wrapped in Jag's arms, the distant thunder roll made Jag feel drowsy. The rain would help him fall asleep, while he pondered how he could make Ethan's Halloween truly terrifying.

6

FEELIN' FROGGY

Ethan had been living with his demon boyfriend for nine months.

During that time, they both had learned a lot about each other and their cultures. Jag was still struggling with conflict resolution that didn't end up with someone's head on a spike, but had taken to human food, music, and art very well. Jag was a man of simple tastes and strong opinions but was willing to try anything once.

Ethan had also learned to oblige certain demon customs that were...a little out of his comfort zone.

For example, Jag insisted that proper gifts should be given outside of clumps of dirt and processed sugar and had brought more than one skull home. The first one was a bull skull because Jag was very impressed with the horns that grew out of the same meat they consumed for burgers. A well-stacked, medium-rare burger was Jag's favorite thing, so finding out that the source of his delight had horns was fantastic.

Naturally, that meant he *had* to gift one to Ethan. When questioned on where he got the skull, Jag only mentioned that it wasn't a defeat he would add to his roster.

When Ethan explained that slaying an animal and defleshing

its head wasn't as championed on earth as it was back in Jag's world, Ethan saw the look of disappointment in his eyes. So Ethan made him a "do's" and "don'ts" list of what animals were acceptable for...gifting.

Ethan wanted to nip that in the bud fast before Jag showed up proudly holding a rhino skull, and Ethan would have to murder him for the honor of all endangered species.

As it was, Ethan had nine skulls, one per month, that were placed with care on his dresser in the bedroom that ran the gamut of sizes. Jag was very proud of them. Ethan prayed no one ever saw in his bedroom.

The other thing Ethan had learned was that he was a bit more sexually adventurous than he thought he was. Not that Ethan wasn't a daring guy given the chance and would have had way more experience under his belt if he had been a *little* more brave about dating in his twenties, but sleeping with a demon was a whole different experience.

Jag was hungry. All the time. For Ethan. And he never allowed them to do the same thing more than once, unless it was something Ethan wanted. It was wonderful, and intimidating, and thrilling, and *intimidating.* Jag had centuries of sexcapades logged away with various other demons and whatever else lived in his realm.

Ethan had one serious boyfriend of three years who dumped him and an awkward virginity story he never cared to revisit.

So yeah.

Not quite Champion of the Blood Wars-level notches in his belt.

But it was getting there. He was getting his notches.

A lot.

Like, a whole lot.

Daily.

All over the house.

And once in an IKEA parking lot—but they had a sale, and Ethan was really excited about his new shelf.

Ethan's life was pretty amazing, and they had settled into something close to a normal domestic routine. Jag's warm hands on Ethan's shoulders as he finished up breakfast was a sensation he'd come to look forward to each morning, as was Jag's lips against his neck.

"Morning, Ethan."

Ethan leaned back into Jag's chest, lifting his chin for a kiss while he continued to scramble the eggs. "Morning, Jag."

"The sky seems green this morning."

"Green?" Ethan glanced towards the windows above the sink. It was dark outside, the storm mentioned on Ethan's phone when he got up this morning. The rolling thunderstorm predicted was supposed to be a doozy, but Ethan didn't remember seeing anything about it being "green."

"I don't know if it's green, but it's definitely dark." Ethan set the pan aside to grab plates, but the wall of half-dressed Jag behind him blocked his path. Freshly showered, Jag smelled like the spicy, musky body wash he had preferred, his skin a little too warm to be natural. The charm around his neck, the thing that kept his human façade in place, was between his fingers.

Jag lifted one brow, a smirk tugging at his lips.

"I was thinking about you in the shower this morning, Ethan."

"Oh?" Ethan swallowed the excited knot that formed in his throat at seeing Jag's eyes swirl in molten shades. The pendant twisting in Jag's fingers made his human skin shimmer and tease at what was hiding beneath. Because Ethan was a master at flirting and dominating a sexy situation, he seductively said, "The eggs will get cold."

One of Jag's large, predatory hands slipped under Ethan's sweatpants to grab a palm full of his cheek. "I'll take my nourishment elsewhere."

"Jesus." Ethan allowed himself to be manhandled away from

the stove and only flounder a little as Jag hefted him up off the ground by his hips onto the counter. The cold tile of the kitchen counter was a brutal contrast to the pouring heat from the demon in front of him, his body a furnace between Ethan's legs. A hungry, very talented tongue slipped into Ethan's mouth, coaxing desperate noises from him that should have been embarrassing.

Jag's hair was wet as Ethan threaded his fingers through it, pulling Jag closer to claim more of him. The shudder through the demon as Ethan lightly raked his nails across his scalp was a drug, and Ethan grinned into Jag's reaction.

"Ethan," Jag breathed into his mouth, the demon voice clawing its way to the surface. "I wish to taste you."

Damn if Ethan didn't just melt onto the counter at that moment. Words were a luxury he couldn't formulate, so he answered by kissing the hungry demon again and gripping his hair in a silent show of dominance. Jag shivered again, and Ethan felt like he could have conquered the world.

Jag's lips and teeth travelled down from Ethan's mouth to his jaw, trailing down with nips and kisses. Ethan slipped his shirt off over his head, throwing it into the sink to allow Jag more access to his skin, when the storm finally moved in. In the very back of Ethan's mind, somewhere lost in the fog of how good Jag's tongue felt slithering over his chest, he noted that the rain sounded a little *off*.

It sounded heavy.

Almost solid.

Ethan was lifting his hips to let Jag tug his sweatpants off when the first frog slapped into the window with a wet thud.

Then another.

And another.

"What the fuck?" Ethan breathed out as he watched his kitchen window crawling with little wet frogs, bouncing up from the ground and covering the view. Jag's fingertips tracing down his thighs made him moan.

"Still concerned about the eggs?" Jag's eyes twinkled as he wiped his lips and Ethan exhaled an embarrassed laugh.

"Not so much. The frogs, on the other hand—"

The sudden, alarming crack of thunder made him jump, and his attention snapped back to the storm. Tiny, slippery bodies of moss-colored frogs were dripping off of his window. The chorus of their throaty songs was almost as loud as the rain outside.

Ethan jerked his sweatpants back on and walked around the kitchen counter to the backdoor, gasping at the horror show outside.

"What the hell!" Ethan covered his mouth, nearly gagging at the sight of tiny frogs raining from the sky. "Jag, what the *hell*?!"

"What?" Jag peered outside, his voice way too casual. "Is this not common?"

"Raining frogs? No!" Ethan peered up at the calming storm, the green clouds starting to ease back to a normal gray. "Why would you think this is normal?"

"Frozen water rains from the sky yearly and coats everything it touches. How is *that* normal, but frogs aren't?" Jag shrugged.

"Does it rain creatures where you're from?" Ethan shot back defensively, then felt stupid for asking when Jag nodded. "Of course it does."

"Not these creatures. Usually, it's flame fins or magma jumpers. They rain down after volcanic irritation."

Ethan wasn't sure how to respond to the idea of that, so he remained silent. The siren songs of hundreds of frogs filled the quiet, as the pair looked out over Ethan's bouncing, green landscape.

The internet was unhelpful when it came to finding any type of explanation. Ethan tapped away on his phone, absently eating cold eggs, while trying to think of various ways to look up, "a cartoon amount of frogs raining from the sky." Even the local news channel only remarked on the event as "a strong spike in frog population," which made Ethan snort egg out of his nose.

Hell of an understatement.

Olivia seemed confused when Ethan sent her a text asking about the storm of frogs, asking politely if he had mixed magic mushrooms into his eggs.

Ethan checked the expiration date on the eggs just to make sure, before sending her a picture of his backyard. She was less teasing then and said she'd help him do some research.

"I dunno who you pissed off, but something is mad at you," she had mentioned. "I'd say light some sage but...yeah. Maybe don't. Also, tell Jag hi."

The question of what could be mad at Ethan was a hysterical one. He was cohabitating with a demon he frequently sinned with on a daily basis. He was fairly sure that meant everything was mad at him. But Ethan, being a man of science and a secular human, didn't follow the thread of any specific superstition to look for answers.

There had to be a scientific and logical explanation as to why buckets of Kermit's family members were now hanging out in his backyard.

He just wasn't sure where to start.

7

COD-BLOCKED

Jag watched as Ethan was gently nudging frogs off of his driveway with a broom.

"I don't believe they will stop your car." Jag waited by the open garage. "They seem to be very small and frail. Your wheels will roll over them."

"Yeah, that's what I'm trying to avoid," Ethan called back, guiding a bouncing creature back into the grass. "I don't want to murder a bunch of little frogs."

"Are they sacred? Is this one of the animals you demand I don't slay for you?"

"Yes, please. I like frogs. Maybe not...this many of them, since this is probably going to be horrible for the ecosystem, but I still feel bad squishing them with my car."

Jag couldn't help but smile at the gentle human trying to wrangle the fussy amphibians bouncing around in his yard. As he watched Ethan whittling away at his patience for the small creatures, the air beside him twisted like a ripple in water. The small passageway between the human realm and Jag's home parted, and Sami slipped through nimbly, the door sealing shut behind him as quickly as it had opened.

"Good morning, Master." Sami's long, green ears perked as he listened to the frogs.

"Sami. We are about to depart, and you know it stresses Ethan out when you're not in disguise."

"Oh, yes." Sami flipped the hood up on his sweater, and Jag nodded in approval. "I need to discuss something with you, Master."

Jag glanced up at Ethan at the far end of the driveway, chasing a family of frogs out of the street. He motioned for Sami to step into the garage with him, and they retreated back near the stored winter decorations and old paint cans.

Jag motioned for Sami to continue.

"Your presence is being requested by the war clan leaders, Master. The alliance between the Blackclaw and Skullsplinter clans are breaking down. The Bonereaver clan has been summoned to hold positions in case of war."

"They're always about to be at war," Jag complained, annoyed to his very core. "They bicker like bratty children every century. It's tiresome."

"The upcoming Hallow's Eve has everyone anxious." Sami wrung his little hands together. "They seem convinced this year will bring about something spectacular."

"Each year, they promise we will have a grand victory that will have Satan himself stepping off his throne. This year will be no different." Jag dismissed the concern with a casual wave.

"Regardless, as their champion, you've been asked to be ready for battle. I keep explaining to them that you're training, but I don't know how much longer I can stall." Sami's wide, worried obsidian eyes blinked up at Jag. "We might need a plan."

"What plan?" Jag gestured around the garage. "I'm bound here. I'm stuck."

"Yes." Sami swallowed and lowered his long, pointy ears. "A violation of human/demon treaty such as unlawful summoning without a license is reason enough for them to get a permit, Master. With a permit, they could come get you."

Jag stared at his familiar. "What are you saying?"

"You know the clans better than I do. What would they do if they found out a human was holding you hostage?"

Jag set his jaw, rage curling in his gut like white-hot flames. "If they come here with the means to harm Ethan, they will not survive my wrath."

"There's no doubt in my mind you'd be victorious, Master. But this would only complicate things further. This could mean more permits, and the rescue mission would shift to being a display of treason." Sami fidgeted. "We need a plan."

Jag's anger cooled into icy dread. Demons coming into the human world was problematic at best. At worst, it would be an excuse for war. Jag was honored to be the clans' champion, and nine months ago, he couldn't have hesitated a moment to join them for battle.

That was before being dragged to the human world. Before learning about cookies, facing the torturous snow, understanding the concepts of romance like flowers and misshapen hearts hung on strings.

That was before Ethan.

"We do need a plan," Jag admitted, his voice deflating with each word. "Give me some time to think. Today, I'm helping Ethan prepare for the human's version of Hallow's Eve, so I cannot focus on the clan's petty problems."

"Yes, Master." Sami nodded his head quickly, his long ears lifting ever so slightly. "Is there going to be a battle, orgy, and feast?"

"Sadly, no. They decorate with fake body parts and costumes." Jag glanced towards the driveway, then leaned down to whisper, "I need you to find me a traditional costume as a surprise for Ethan."

"Yes, Master." Sami nodded, his ears bobbing. "Whatever you wish."

"I need you to find the armor of the Power Rangers. This is vital. The gloves must make noises as well."

Sami gave a slow nod. "What sort of noises?"

"Wind noises."

His familiar pondered for a moment, wringing his hands. "I'll see what I can find, Master."

"I think that's as good as it's going to get," Ethan said with a long sigh as he marched his way back up the driveway. "I'll just try and back out slowly."

"If they stray into your path, Ethan, they aren't meant to procreate. Sami, begone. We must depart."

"Yes, Master. Have a good day preparing for merriment." Sami gave Ethan a polite wave and slipped back between the realms.

"Everything okay? Sami seemed fidgety." Ethan walked around to the driver's side and entered the car. Jag did the same on the passenger's side.

"He is a familiar. They are 'fidgety' by nature."

Ethan cut Jag a stern look that was too kind to have any real edge. "You know what I mean."

"He worries about my absence back home."

"Is something going on?" Ethan dared a quick look Jag's direction before focusing back on not murdering frogs with his car.

"No more than usual." Jag rotated backward to watch through the back window as Ethan tried to navigate through the bouncing obstacles. He did fairly well, but there was one distinct squish that made Ethan groan.

The building Ethan took them to seemed like any other in the strip of businesses within the shopping center. Large lettering across the building had long been removed, but the ghostly silhouette helped Jag to identify that it used to be a toy store. Instead of a permanent sign, there was a large canvas sign flapping above the door, proclaiming the new territory under the banner of Halloween Plus.

Spiderwebs made of stretched cotton covered the glass door around the "Open If You Dare" sign hanging by a small plastic suction cup. Ethan grinned as metal pumpkins hanging from the handle jingled upon their entry.

There was a lot to process when Jag entered Halloween Plus. By the front door, a large fake spider wiggled at them threateningly, which caused Ethan to jump and laugh. Jag noted that the large arachnid had two glowing red eyes, which was an odd choice, given the creature had many more. Plastic bats hung motionless in the air, their wings stuck outstretched while they spun in lazy circles.

Towering figures of metal, cloth, and plastic crafted to resemble various human concepts of monsters, death, and even demons flailed around screaming in electronic voices. They were in fact not filled with cheese, as Ethan had previously hinted at. Only common materials and electric wiring.

It was the funniest thing Jag had ever seen.

Satan was human-sized with comically small horns. Ghosts were fully clothed. Werewolves stood upright. Vampires looked like humans. Death was personified as a sentient skeleton, which any self-respecting demon knew was the easiest foe to defeat. Bumbling, skinless corpses were training material for infants, nothing threatening about them.

Ludicrous. Hilarious.

"You seem to be enjoying yourself," Ethan remarked as Jag examined a cake mold of a human brain.

"This is all so ridiculous. Is this what humans think we look like?" He gestured to the robot Satan, who was demanding patrons have a "Happy Halloween."

"This is kind of the satire version of it. These aren't really meant to be scary."

"I certainly hope not." Jag set the mold aside and drifted over to the rows and rows of crimson-filled jugs nearby. The liquid inside seemed syrupy and deep red, and Jag was impressed upon seeing the label.

"Ethan, how do they keep these containers of blood from rotting?" Jag hoisted a gallon of blood up by its convenient handle and unscrewed it, taking a careful sniff. "...Ethan, this smells like sugar. This is not blood. Who is peddling such lies?" Jag cringed as he tasted it, spitting to the side.

"It's fake, Jag." Ethan took the jug away and screwed the lid back on. "We can't actually buy real blood, remember?"

Jag did remember because he had planned on trying to cook for Ethan one night. Those dreams had been dashed.

Beyond the hanging fake body parts, the comically blunt and easily breakable plastic swords, were the aisles of Halloween costumes. Jag enjoyed every second of browsing the garments made for the holiday, admiring the smattering of the "ghoulish" and the sexy versions of the ghoulish. There were confusing articles of clothing, like giant food items, costumes shaped like genitalia, or references to movies he hadn't seen yet. Whoever Joe Exotic was offended Jag to his very core.

Ethan loaded up a shopping cart with various items needed for the home: the cotton webbing, fake spiders, lights in the shape of pumpkins, some articulated skeletons, and jugs of "fog juice," which Jag was completely confused by. Along with the decorations, a box containing one of the wiggling biclops arachnid was also purchased.

"I think this is a good start," Ethan remarked as he loaded the items into the trunk. "I think next we should find some tombstones and maybe a ghoul to hang from the tree."

"I thought you didn't want it to be too scary?" Jag asked as he climbed into the passenger seat.

"Maybe a *little* scary. Just not 'horrify children until their dying days' scary. Somewhere in between works." A playful smirk tugged at his lips. "I also grabbed something kinda fun."

Jag lifted his eyebrow as Ethan sat in the driver's seat and dug through a plastic bag. After a couple seconds of him fighting with a small plastic bag, a headband slipped over his hair to rest across his skull.

Red fabric covered the small band that pressed into his hair, with two small devil horns popping up from the top in a lazy curl. They were tiny and matched the red that bloomed across Ethan's cheeks as he cracked a full grin.

"Taa-daa! What do you think of my horns?"

Jag was a man who was not easily impressed. He had conquered feral chaos boars during hunts, slayed countless warriors in battle, bedded all manner of lovers from fellow demons to the creature species that dwelled in his land. Centuries of debauchery and unabashed sexcapades made Jag a seasoned professional of desire and pleasure.

But nothing was as sexy as Ethan in fake devil horns.

"Satan," Jag breathed out. "Did you just buy those?"

"Yeah?" Ethan laughed, sounding nervous. "Are you okay?"

"How fast can you get us home?"

The red in Ethan's cheeks spread to his neck. "Seriously? This is doing it for you?"

"Yes. Oh, Satan, *yes.*"

"Uh. Oh. Uh." Ethan dropped his keys, cussed, then tried to fish them off the floor. "Like ten minutes?"

"That's too long."

"Jag—oh my God." Ethan tensed as his seat was pushed backwards, blinking up in surprise as Jag leaned over him. "We're in public!"

"This has not stopped us before." Jag grinned over his sweet human as Ethan's skin erupted into more shades of red. "We didn't get a chance to enjoy ourselves this morning. And I need to feel you right now."

"Damn," Ethan exhaled. "If I knew ninety-eight-cent horns were going to turn you on, I would have gotten more."

"Never take them off," Jag growled into the supple skin of Ethan's neck, nipping his teeth up his jaw. "I want to see your face light up with pleasure while I taste you with my tongues."

Whatever words Ethan tried to speak were trapped in his throat, and Jag drank in the desperate noise that quivered out. It had been expressed early in the relationship that sex in public was a social taboo, and something Ethan was reluctant to engage in again. The sweet human was terribly shy, which added to his deliciousness, and Jag enjoyed coaxing him into breaking the rules.

Ethan made sure to let Jag know that was very like the human concept of demons. Apparently, they're known for being tempting.

Jag liked that. He would never get tired of tempting Ethan in provocative ways.

Ethan's fingers threaded through Jag's hair, his pulse rapid fire against Jag's one human tongue. He wouldn't shift yet, not when Ethan was still unsure. Once he had Ethan writhing and begging, he'd pull forward his demon form to properly devour his sweet human. The teasing was half the fun.

The firm ridge pressing into Jag's palm as he slid his hand between Ethan's legs made Jag grin, and there was no resistance when he popped Ethan's jeans open.

"Oh my God, this is so illegal." Ethan's voice was battling between worry and arousal. "What if someone sees us?"

"Good for them." Jag slipped his fingers around Ethan's cock and squeezed. "You're beautiful when you come."

Ethan's eyebrows lifted in pleasure, his bottom lip catching between his teeth. Satan, he really was beautiful when he was enjoying himself. Pale cheeks flushed red, dark lashes over his cheeks, those cute little horns on his head. Jag felt his body burning from the inside out, his heart hammering against his ribs, flesh aching to press against Ethan's.

Jag was so busy trying to calculate how he could position

them in a way that he could fuck Ethan in the car that he missed the rolling thunder. Ethan's captivating expressions and sweet noises distracted him from noticing the darkening clouds. The hot, firm flesh in his palm was too enticing for Jag to realize that something evil was brewing.

Just as Jag started toying with the charm, eager to wrap his tongues around the panting human under his spell, it began to rain.

Only it wasn't raining water.

Or frogs.

The sound of a meaty body landing on the car's hood jerked them both back to reality. Ethan yelped in alarm as his horn went off, the warped sound of metal denting under pressure warbling through the air. Jag extracted himself from Ethan's pants, staring in confusion at the familiar shape of the creature on the hood.

The thunder was growing distant as they climbed out of the car, their eyes glued to the dead animal lying across the dented, slightly scorched metal. What was once a flaming fin along the back of the black scaled fish was now just a boney, broken sail. Black ichor oozed from its open mouth lined with daggers, the void-like eyes wide and empty.

"Is that…" Ethan paused, trying to make sense of what he was seeing. "A...shark?"

Jag scowled.

"A shark on fire?" Ethan added, his voice growing more tilted with panic.

"No," Jag corrected. "It's a magma jumper."

Ethan slowly turned towards Jag, his face snow-white. "Like from where you're from?"

"Yes."

"Are you sure?" Ethan shook his head, looking back at the dead, hellish creature. "Of course you're sure. What am I saying?" He ran both hands over his face, pausing with his fingers over his mouth. "How is it here?"

"I don't know, Ethan." Jag inspected the sky, which was starting to brighten again. "Something is wrong."

"Yeah. Something is very, very wrong." They continued to stare at the dead fish for a long, tense moment before Ethan added, "I think we're going to need some help."

"Help?"

"Uh-huh." Ethan handed Jag an old sweater from his backseat. "I'm scared of touching that. Can you pick it up?"

"Who could possibly help us?" Jag grabbed the fish by the tail and hefted it up, allowing Ethan to wrap it up in a sweater and toss it into the trunk.

"The only person I know with even the slightest bit of magic knowledge."

"You mean the witch?" Jag stepped back as Ethan gagged.

"Yeah." Ethan nodded quickly. "Olivia."

8

SIDE ORDER OF AWFUL

This was bad.

The frogs were weird and unsettling to say the least, but the last incident was the demonic flaming shark that broke the camel's back. Whatever was going on was way out of their scope, and they needed to call in an expert.

Sadly, Ethan didn't know anyone who was an authority on the occult, demons, or animals raining from the sky, but he did have something close. He had a witch.

"Olivia said she can come over tonight for dinner." Ethan allowed himself to breathe in relief for a moment before a new brick of dread started to form. "Jag, I think we're going to have to tell her about you."

"Why?" Jag's eyes were glued to the sky, searching for any signs of continued zoological weather patterns.

"If she's going to help us understand what's going on, then she needs all the information." Ethan rubbed at his stomach, which was bubbling in anxiety. "This is so bad."

Jag growled but tilted his head in agreement. "Understandable. But I don't like it."

"Trust me. I don't either." The headache forming in his

temples was like feeling a vice grip across his skull, but Ethan ignored it. He had to figure out something to make for dinner, while ignoring the terrifying possibility that the fabric of reality was tearing.

It made landing on a recipe very difficult.

Jag kept his post by the window, keeping watch over the landscape while Ethan bustled around the kitchen in a mad frenzy of stress cooking. By the time Olivia arrived for dinner, Ethan had made so many side dishes that he ran out of counter space, and the rolls were a little burnt.

He also forgot to cook a main dish.

"Wow, you are having a day." Olivia raised her eyebrows at the cacophony of side dishes scattered around the kitchen. "Did you get news back about your job or something?"

"What? No." Ethan shook his head, cheeks flushing. "Why would you think that?"

"Because the only time you make twenty sides is when you're extremely stressed out. When they put you on sabbatical, you made four pies, remember?"

"That was a good day," Jag said over his shoulder.

"It's nothing like that." Ethan pulled the burnt rolls out and scowled at them. "I'm not stressed."

"Okay." Olivia snort-laughed through her words and grabbed a plate. "Go sit down. Jag, make your man a plate of sides."

Ethan was ushered out of the kitchen and waited at the table he forgot to set. Jag brought him a plate piled with food, since demons had no impulse control, and Olivia brought in utensils and drinks. Unlike Jag, who had finished a plate and gone back for seconds, Ethan could barely manage to eat anything. Olivia's eyes skimmed his plate, then lifted to stare at him.

"Ethan. What's wrong?"

"Okay." Ethan exhaled, rubbing both hands over his face. "This is...going to sound insane and weird, but Jag and I need to talk to you about something."

"Uh-huh." Olivia set her fork down and waited, glancing towards Jag, who was still eating.

"It's, um...well, Jag and I...God, where do I start?"

Olivia exhaled deeply and gave a slow nod. "I think I know what's going on here."

"I really don't think you do." Ethan rubbed his aching stomach. "I really don't know how to say it, Olivia, but Jag is—"

"Ethan. I've been in this situation before." Olivia lifted her hand. "It explains the millions of side dishes and your stomach."

"You've...been in *what* situation before?" Ethan hedged.

"We can be adults about this." She shrugged her shoulders lazily. "You and Jag invited me here for a threesome."

Ethan sputtered, his soul trying to escape his body from embarrassment. Jag lifted his head in mid-chew, eyebrows raised.

"Olivia!" Ethan voice had taken a pterodactyl screech tone he was not proud of. "No!"

"Okay, sorry!" She waved her hands to try and expel the discomfort from the situation. "Misread the situation! You don't have to sound *that* horrified, by the way."

"You've 'been in this situation before?' With who? When?! How often?!"

"None of your business and shut up." Olivia crossed her arms definitely. "Then what the hell is your deal? What's going on?"

"Wait, we're not having a threesome?" Jag asked around a mouthful of food.

"Oh my God." Ethan buried his face in his hands, wishing he could crawl under the table.

"Are you two engaged?" The question made Ethan groan in agony.

"Engaged in what?" Jag asked, growing more confused.

"I take that as a no." Olivia drummed her fingers on the table. "Having a baby?"

The question nearly slapped Ethan out of his chair.

"What?" Jag snapped his eyes to Ethan. "You told me you can't get pregnant."

"Oh my *God.*" Ethan sank lower on the table.

Jag leaned over to Ethan, his whispering skills beyond terrible. "Ethan, do human ribs retract? Because we are birthed through the torso, and I'm concerned for your narrow frame."

"Jag, please." Ethan said into his folded arms. "I'm not pregnant. It's fine."

"Oh, thank Satan."

"Then *what*, Ethan? What's up?" Olivia tried again, glancing between the two of them.

Ethan exhaled and tossed his hands up in exasperation. "Jag's a demon. And I think we're causing the apocalypse."

Olivia leveled him with an icy look of a woman scorned. "Me asking if you wanted a threesome is not the end of days, you twat."

"No, I mean Jag is literally a demon. Do you remember the book I was translating from? I summoned him by accident right before Christmas."

"Is that why they put you on sabbatical? They have a strict 'no summoning demons' rule?" she teased, her smirk falling when Ethan winced. "Oh, Ethan, I was just kidding."

"They put me on sabbatical because they didn't believe me when I said the language was linked to the occult." Ethan rubbed at the sting in his chest. "But I'm telling the truth."

Olivia's eyes swung from Ethan to Jag. "I don't know what to say right now."

"Jag can show you, but…" Ethan swallowed and held his stomach. "Try not to freak out? I know that's not fair to ask because it's going to be really freaky."

The placating slow nod from Olivia would have been hilarious in any other circumstance, but Ethan was on the verge of collapsing in on himself like a dying star. Ethan gave Jag *the nod*, and Jag finished the last bite of food.

Raising from the table, Jag took his shirt off and tossed it into the seat. He had changed into sweatpants to allow for the stretch to his size, and Olivia blinked at Jag's bare chest.

"You guys sure you're not about to ask me—OH MY GOD." Olivia jumped from the table as Jag removed the charm around his neck, his body expanding out into his full demon shape. His skin melted into its natural deep red tone, his curled black horns sprouting and reshaping from his skull. Jag had to stretch out his jaw some to adjust to the extra molars that formed in his mouth and resituate his dexterous tongue.

Or tongues, rather.

Olivia was frozen in place, her hands locked over her mouth as if to hold in her shock. Ethan had never seen her eyes so big, and he noted that she had stopped blinking completely.

"Olivia?" Ethan came to stand by her, worried she'd faint. "You okay?"

"Oh my *God.* How...how is this happening? Is this real?"

"I assure you, I am very real." Jag plucked a burned roll off Ethan's plate and took a bite.

"Holy shit." Olivia watched Jag eating bread like the otherworldly creature he was. "Is the threesome offer still on the table?"

"Olivia!"

"I don't know what I'm saying!" She gestured wildly at Jag. "Look at him!"

"I am surprised at how willing humans are to have sex with a demon." Jag stuffed the last of the roll in his mouth. "I thought you were afraid of us."

Ethan laughed. "Who do you think got me into Jex Lane?" He jerked his thumb over to Olivia.

"I'm not an Incubus," Jag deadpanned at Olivia before she could ask. She looked disappointed.

"Ethan, I appreciate that you thought of me when it came to the occult, but I'm not that sort of witch." Olivia's face was morphing from pure awe over Jag to transparent worry. "I'm a green witch. Sage, crystals, smudge sticks, the occasional tarot readings, but not this. Not the dark arts and demons. That is really scary stuff."

"I know, and I'm sorry we've pulled you into this, but you're all we've got." Ethan made prayer hands in front of himself to drive his desperation home. "Please, Olivia."

"Okay. Okay." Olivia ran her fingers through her black hair. "You summoned a demon."

Ethan nodded. "Yes."

"Who's now your boyfriend," she continued.

Ethan's cheeks warmed. "Correct."

"And you think you're causing the end of days?"

Jag went to get more bread. "Precisely."

"Oh, shit. The frogs." Olivia tapped her head in an "of course" gesture. "Yeah, that makes sense now. That's some Biblical shit, Ethan. You pissed off whoever's in charge with your unholy union."

"That wasn't the worst one—" Ethan jumped as Jag hefted the dead Flame Fin shark from the freezer and dumped it onto the table. The flame was out of course, but the frozen, gaping mouth of a demonic shark made Olivia yell in alarm.

"That is...*badass!*" She leaned over it in amazement. "Is this a fucking demon shark?!"

"Of course you think this is badass." Ethan rubbed at his temples.

"It's a fish from my world. It fell on Ethan's car." Jag pushed it towards Olivia. "You can keep it. I don't care for their meat."

"Don't." Ethan shook his head. "Don't eat it. It'll probably kill you."

"Noted." She grinned and looked the dead nightmare over before refocusing back on the odd couple pleading for help. "Both of these happened today?"

demon. There was no way Ethan would ever be able to kiss a guy with only one tongue again.

Jag broke the kiss before it could get too steamy, but Ethan had already slipped his hand up to cup Jag's cheek for more. The demon's chuckle made Ethan blush.

"Easy, human." Jag swiped his thumb under Ethan's lip. "I'll make sure you're taken care of later."

Ethan's poor, stressed heart was going to fall out of his chest from how sexy Jag was.

The crack of thunder made him jump and break contact with Jag, but not before they got the beginning sprinkles of the threatening storm.

"Is that hail?" Olivia slipped around them to peer out the glass patio door by the kitchen. The clouds had begun to melt away as Ethan put more distance between him and Jag, following Olivia to see what was falling from the sky.

His stomach tightened as he cringed. "Are those...snails?"

"Yeah." Olivia plucked one off the ground. "Black snails."

"Obsidian," Jag added as one of the tiny creatures landed in his palm. A small, inky-black snail poked its little head free and started its long, slow climb up Jag's massive thumb. "This is made of rock."

"Great. Something else from your world." Ethan scowled at the tiny creature sliding around on Jag's skin. "At least it wasn't a shark this time."

"These aren't from my world." Jag shook his head. "I don't know what these are."

"I would wager to guess it's a mixture of both worlds," Olivia explained as she set her snail down outside. She dusted her hands off and turned towards the two men watching the black rock snail. "Until we figure out how this is happening, the two of you aren't allowed to touch each other."

"No." Jag didn't even lift his head as he spoke, too mesmerized by the gastropod.

"You two touching is what's causing the storms." Olivia crossed her arms in the cocky, winner posture of a witch who knew what she was talking about. "Each time you two get too close or get 'hot and bothered,' something terrible happens. I feel like if you screw right now, you'd summon Satan."

"Satan himself cannot keep me from Ethan," Jag growled. "Let him come."

"That's sweet and badass, but I think that would also mean the end of the world, Jag. Which means the end of Ethan." Her observation made Jag scowl.

"Jag, she's right." Ethan reached out to place a hand on Jag's arm, remembered himself, and pulled back. "We'll need to keep some distance until we find out why this is happening."

"How?" Jag set his jaw. "I don't know dark magic, and the book you used to summon me is locked away at the university."

"I have notes and scanned pages." Ethan let out a sigh. "It's better than nothing."

"We'll start there." She wagged her finger at them as she continued. "Until then, I'm serious. No sexcapades of any kind. Kissing, hugging, over-the-clothes hand stuff, *nothing*. If you two cause the end of the world because you're horny idiots, I'll kill you."

Ethan was fairly sure they were doomed.

9

WILD OATHS

It was surreal to see the pages from the book again, even if they were digitally scanned images on a laptop screen. Ethan had sworn the work off after getting laughed out of the room with his findings. Everyone on the board, including his peers, thought he had lost his mind. His paper about the lost language of an occult society with ties to demonic culture was passed over as another fringe conspiracy theory.

Getting placed on sabbatical wasn't his idea. But it was better than being fired.

That had been two months ago, and Ethan had shoved all of his work in a drawer to rot.

Seeing the pages again was extremely bittersweet, since Jag was still here with him but his academic standing was not. His sprawling notes in his beat-up spiral was the Rosetta Stone for the dead, demonic language, with massive gaps and missing information. Even with a year of studying the strange writing and linguistic maze that was this language, Ethan had only managed to translate a few letters and basic words.

"This is the rough translation of the spell I used." Ethan

smoothed a page out for Olivia to read. "But it's only half of the page."

"Oath of the Heart, huh? I knew you were taking David's breakup hard, but Jesus, Ethan."

"I don't want to talk about it." Ethan angled the laptop screen so Jag could see it. "Can you translate this, Jag?" He tapped the screen, and Jag narrowed his eyes.

"This is not what you read."

"Yeah? I think so. It's not as easy to read on the computer." Ethan rotated the laptop back around to double check.

"That says Vows, not Oath."

The laptop nearly toppled to the floor. "Pardon? Vows?"

"Oh my God, are you two married?" Olivia gasped in delight.

A cold wave of panic set in Ethan's bones. "Did I force you to marry me, Jag?! Oh my *God*."

Jag moved his eyes between the two clearly insane humans. "No. You just have the wrong page."

After a moment to let his blood pressure settle, Ethan realized he had in fact pulled up the wrong page. He was not a monster who pulled some unsuspecting demon out of their world and forced them into an unholy matrimony. He was just a monster who pulled some unsuspecting demon out of their world to make his ex jealous.

And then slept with said demon.

So. That's where he was in life.

Once the correct page was in front of Jag, he tried again to read the text. "I can read it, but I don't understand magic and its rules. I'm a warrior, and we don't use magic. It's cowardly."

"Dark magic is considered cowardly?" Olivia scoffed.

"They're tricks. Unbreakable contracts binding humans and demons together under strict and unforgiving circumstances. This is why we sealed the doors between our realms." Jag jabbed a finger at the screen. "Because humans put us in chains, and we bottled their souls to harness as weapons."

"Weapons?" Ethan leaned forward on his elbows, his imagination running wild. "How?"

Jag snarled as he spoke, as if the words tasted bad in his mouth. "In the wrong hands, life essence can be manipulated into unnatural blights to be unleashed. In the Chasm War, a sorcerer used bottled human souls to liquify and curse an entire clan. It caused our kind to close the doors between the realms. Unless one applies for a permit, of course."

"See? That's awesome," Olivia argued. "How is that not awesome?"

"Battles are won with might, cunning, and strategy, not tricks. We had plans on reclaiming the human realm before The Chasm War, but that battle caused us to splinter and start fighting each other. The human world is off-limits until we can unite."

"That's...unsettling." Ethan couldn't mask the uncomfortable feeling in his stomach from reaching his face. "Does that mean demons are planning on coming to Earth some day?"

"We'll never stop fighting each other, Ethan. I wouldn't worry too much." Jag tapped the screen. "We need to focus on this. I may not know this magic, but Sami does. Familiars know devious tricks and dark arts. Sami!"

"Yes, Master?" Sami slipped from the pocket of reality, his ears flattening the moment his black eyes landed on Olivia. A sharp hiss escaped him as he bared his needle teeth her way, and she yelped in alarm.

"It's fine. She knows," Jag said casually, and his tiny, green companion melted back into his normal, fidgety, friendly self.

Sami's long, elf-like ears perked up. "Hello!"

"What the shit?" Olivia huffed, her hand pressed against her heart to keep it from leaping from her chest. "Where did he come from?"

"I guess technically hell?" Ethan offered. "Though I don't think that's what they call their realm."

Jag slid the laptop over to Sami. "You don't have enough tongues to pronounce our realm."

"Hot," Olivia tagged on, ignoring Ethan's sharp glare. Sami's ears lifted as his dark eyes skipped over the screen, his lips muttering words silently as he made sense of what he was seeing.

"This is the oath Ethan used on you, Master."

"Yes. We're trying to decipher why things are falling from the sky when we get too close to each other. The oath must explain conditions to our contract, correct?" Jag tapped the screen. "How can we stop this annoying inconvenience?"

"Falling from the sky?" Sami's large, inky eyes somehow widened, his ears flexing out to the side. "Like what?"

"Frogs and a magma jumper so far." Ethan shivered. "And some creepy rock snails."

"Oh, no." Sami's ears dropped. "This is bad."

"Why?" Jag's scowl cut his features. "What does this mean?"

Sami's normal fidgeting was something Ethan was used to. The small, green, goblin-looking entity that catered to Jag's every whim was in a constant state of fretting as it was. Even if Jag was pleased, Sami always looked like he was ready to fall to the ground groveling. But the mention of the animals plummeting to the sky made Sami turn full shaking chihuahua as he rolled his hands around like a terrified mouse.

"You've caused rifts, Master. Each oath has set conditions based on the type of magic used. For this instance, the magic that pulled you into the human realm must be very strong and caused small tears in the fabric between worlds." Sami began mimicking tearing paper in half with his hands. "Each of these holes gets bigger the longer the oath is in place."

"So." Ethan hedged, trying to ignore the sour knot forming in his gut. "Is that how the magma jumper got through? What about the frogs? Those are from this world. And the snails are from neither world."

Sami shook his head, forming a circle with his hands. "The

tears don't just allow physical things though, but magic as well. Much more dangerous. Demon magic is leaking through, causing flux within your world."

"Why would the holes get bigger each time we are physically touching? Don't." Ethan pointed a finger at Olivia. "This is serious."

She winked and mouthed the words, *That's what he said.*

"Because of the nature of the oath." Sami made an X over his heart. "Love and revenge magic is strongest. This oath is both of those, which means it punched through the veil between worlds and is eating away at it slowly."

"How do we stop it?" Jag tapped the laptop screen. "What does it say?"

"You stop it by completing the contract, Master. You have to finish the task so a doorway home can open to you." Sami crossed his arms in front of him at the wrist. "A demon cannot stay in this realm by a tether of magic. Even permits only last so long before walls start breaking down. You need to go home, or the holes will start letting more things through."

"Is that...the only option?" Ethan's stomach twisted. "Jag has to leave?"

"No." Jag shook his head, curling his fist. "I will not be chased home because of ancient magic. There are always loopholes and conditions. We just need to find them."

"Master is correct," Sami agreed with a quick nod. "There are sometimes ways to bend the magic in our favor. The book you read from is very old and one of the very rare books containing spells and oaths made by human and demon cooperation. If anything has the answer to fixing this, it's the book."

"Then we have no time to waste. Sami, translate everything you can from this computer. Ethan scanned the pages." Jag pointed to the computer, and Sami quickly got to work.

"I'll help you go over the notes, Ethan," Olivia chimed in.

"Maybe you missed something before. An extra set of eyes can't hurt."

Cautious relief started to bloom in Ethan's chest. "Thanks, Olivia."

"We'll fix this." Jag tried to touch his hand, only remembering the restrictions when Ethan pulled away.

The hurt in Jag's eyes was almost too much to bear.

———

By the time Sami had translated the digital pages, Ethan and Olivia had fallen asleep, and Jag had a throbbing headache. Hours had passed, and each of them had pored over notes to try and find any scrap of information that would assist. Ethan's soft breathing moved the pages of his notebook, his head resting across folded arms.

Months ago, when Ethan had come home from the university without a job, Jag witnessed firsthand how badly stress tore him down. Ethan stopped eating, slept for days, complained about stomach pains, and gave up on doing much else beyond existing. It had taken weeks to pull Ethan from his despair, but shadows of it haunted him on occasion.

Seeing Ethan ignore his dinner of side dishes and fall asleep on his notebook were chilly reminders of those days. It lit a fire in Jag to keep hunting, desperate to find an answer to keep the world from falling apart.

And make Ethan feel better.

Sami rubbed at his eyes, his ears limp around his face. "Master, I have unfortunate news."

"I don't want to hear it." Jag pressed the skin between his brows, trying to force the headache into submission. "There's no time for unfortunate news."

"I've gone over the pages countless times, but there is information missing. There are other spells, oaths, and pledges that are similar, but the Oath of the Heart is missing elements. Ethan must have missed parts of the passages when he was scanning them in." Sami's clawed fingertip scratched carefully at the laptop screen. "See there? It cuts off right in the middle of the oath. It's incomplete."

"This is not optimal." Jag's eyes were gritty as he pressed his fingers against his eyelids.

"Does Ethan still have access to the book?" Sami's ears perked, then deflated as Jag shook his head.

"The university forced him to take time off, remember? He does not have access anymore."

"I see." Sami drummed his claws against the desk. "What do we do now, Master?"

The question hung in the air like a foul stench. The only key they had to repairing the massive tears between their realms was locked away in a university they didn't have access to. Magic was cross-contaminating their worlds, causing terrifying storms of creatures to rain down and cause mayhem. If it wasn't happening to Jag, he would love the idea of something so cataclysmic as frogs raining from the sky.

But as it was, the situation was causing him to lack physical touch with the only person he wanted. So he was very annoyed.

Ethan's soft sigh sent a lance through Jag's heart. He sounded so tired. Forgetting the apocalyptic consequences for a moment, Jag brushed a strand of unruly hair from Ethan's brow and scowled at the distant thunder that threatened.

The demon ground his molars together. "If the book is what we need, then that's what we're going to get."

"Master?" Sami's ears lifted in confusion.

"I want you to break into the university and take the book. Bring it back here through your portal so we can finish this." Jag dismissed his familiar. "Go now."

"Master..." Sami shook his head, hunching his shoulders. "I

cannot bring a tome of that sort of power into my portals. It's too strong. I would burst the moment I tried."

"Satan help me." Jag rubbed his temples. "Of course it couldn't be that easy. Fine. I will ask politely for access to the book out of respect for Ethan because I know the institute means something to him." Jag flexed his hand into a fist to keep himself from stroking Ethan's hair. "But I will not ask a second time. I will gain access to that book and slaughter whoever gets in my way."

"Very heroic, Master." Sami gave a soft round of applause. "Heroic and scary."

Jag pushed himself from the table, careful not to jostle the table and wake Ethan. Snatching a blanket from the back of the couch, Jag draped the faded, soft cloth around the slumbering human. Using the blanket as a barrier, Jag placed his hand over the cloth resting across Ethan's back and waited, listening for thunder. The silence gave him the permission he needed.

Ethan groaned as Jag scooped him up in a blanket cocoon, only his warm breath making contact against Jag's skin. It was painful to have to place the sweet, sleeping human into the bed and not follow, curling up to hold him while he slept.

Instead, Jag made sure he was secure and safe and left to sleep on the couch that was a little too small. He couldn't risk tearing the world apart just to hold him.

No matter how tempting it was.

10

LIBRARY ETIQUETTE

"You want to do what?" Ethan nearly choked on his coffee. It was bad enough waking up alone in bed after suffering through nightmares of raining lava sharks and plagues. His stomach was trying to uncoil itself from the knots formed yesterday, and hearing bad ideas lobbed at him first thing in the morning was having the opposite effect.

"It is our only option." Jag rubbed at his neck, no doubt stiff from sleeping on a couch much too small for him. "We don't have all the pages needed from the book."

"I think Jag's right, Ethan. It's a good idea." Olivia had relocated to the armchair in the middle of the night and slept better than anyone else at the table. Her optimism and cheery attitude that early in the morning was offensive.

"Did you both forget I was basically laughed out of the university because of this book? They're not going to let me borrow it again." Ethan stabbed at his cold oatmeal. "Dr. Hanson used the word 'unhinged.'"

"I will kill him," Jag mumbled into his coffee cup. "I'll unhinge his jaw and snap it off."

"Murder aside, Jag is right," Olivia pressed. "If we don't have all the info, we need to at least try and get access to the book. You have to still have some friends up there that will help you. It's been months."

The oatmeal in Ethan's bowl mocked him as he stirred it. It had smelled so good when he heated it up, but now it was cold and seemed vile. The knots in his guts wouldn't let him eat it anyway.

"I don't know if I can face them again."

"You won't be alone." Olivia tipped her head towards Jag. "You got us. We'll go with you."

"The witch is right." Jag nodded, and Olivia beamed.

"You hear that? The demon called me 'the witch.' I can officially get business cards now."

Ethan let a huff of a laugh bubble through. "You have to promise me, both of you, that you won't cause a scene. I'm not on great terms with them as it is, and I don't want to be...well, *completely* blacklisted. Okay?" He pinned them each with a long stare. Olivia held up her fingers in a scout's honor pose.

Jag crossed his arms. "I promise I will not kill anyone unless you ask."

"And don't yell at anyone. You can be scary."

"I am scary. I'm a demon."

"Jag. Please."

With a pouty huff, the scowly Champion of the Blood Wars agreed.

If seeing the book again had been surreal, then going back to the university was otherworldly.

Ethan hadn't even driven past the front building in months after his exile, the shame of that last day weighing down his soul like a demonic, book-sized albatross. His academic friends had barely reached out, his peers cut ties, and even the book club he was in "conveniently" changed dates and meeting places. Ethan felt like the black sheep, or maybe black goat if he wanted to stay on theme, of the university.

The linguistics building was always quiet in the mornings since classes normally didn't start until closer to eleven. A cool chill always seemed to run through the halls during the colder months, and the smell of dusty books and floor cleaner gave the building a very distinctive smell. The small pang of longing Ethan felt when traveling the halls almost made him double over from heartache, but he kept himself upright.

Unlike the other wings of the university, the linguistics building had its own mini-library with ancient books used in deciphering languages, case studies, foreign language aids, and more. Small rectangles that could barely qualify as windows gave the illusion of lighting, so the humming fluorescents had to do most of the work.

"It smells like a used bookstore here." Olivia did a slow spin as they walked into the library. "Like old paper and dust."

"I know. I love it." Ethan smiled over his shoulder. "This is my favorite place on the entire campus. I spent hours here working on translations before I finally realized the bad lighting and constant humming was giving me migraines."

"Are there other demon tomes here?" Jag sniffed the air and ran his gaze over the wall-to-wall shelving all around them.

"Nothing like the one we're looking for. We have old Bibles and other ancient texts from all over the world, not just Christianity but Hinduism, Islam, even some Buddhist texts that are thousands of years old. It's really amazing." Ethan was so busy gushing about the collection the university housed that he almost ran into the heavy wooden case in the middle of the wide room.

The glass-topped display case housed their rare and important books, a

nd because Ethan had terrible luck and must have angered some deity in his past life, the book they were looking for was locked inside right between a four-hundred-year-old book of poetry and the aforementioned Buddhist text. The demonic book was opened up on display, naturally not on the pages they needed.

"Fuck." Ethan shut his eyes. "Why didn't I think of this? Of course they would put it in here."

"What is this?" Jag tried to move the glass and scowled. "They keep books locked away?"

"They didn't know how old it was until I started researching it. I guess they believed *some* of what I had to say if they had it locked in here."

Olivia put her hands on her hips. "Well this sucks. Who has the key?"

"No one would let me open it." Ethan rubbed his palms into his eyes.

"I'll break the glass, and we can take it." Jag shrugged. "What's the issue?"

"No! God. The other books in this case are extremely fragile. Exposing them to the elements would destroy them."

"They do not matter. We need this book to stop the tears." Jag blinked in surprise when Ethan wagged a finger at him.

"Jagmarith, second son of Bolor'gath, Champion of the Blood Wars, if you harm the books in this case, I will never forgive you."

"Oooh." Olivia covered her mouth. "He whipped out the full name."

Jag cleared his throat, glancing at Olivia, then back to Ethan. "I apologize, Ethan."

"Sorry." The icy flood of embarrassment cooled his fire. "I just don't like the idea of ancient knowledge getting destroyed."

"Nothing to apologize for," Jag purred with a grin. "I like that side of you. Perhaps later we can pretend I harmed a book, and you can punish me."

The ice melted at that, and Ethan felt pinpricks of heat forming along his hairline. His brain tried to think of something to say, but it was a mixture of horny white noise and fluorescent hums.

"Hey." Olivia snapped her fingers. "I'm going to start bringing a spray bottle. Focus. Ethan, how can we safely get into this case?"

"Right. Um." Ethan shook his head, breaking free from the sexy net Jag had thrown over him. "The only people who have access to the keys are the department heads, which are the ones responsible for me leaving. Maybe we can pick the lock?"

"Okay. Do either of you know how to pick a lock?" Olivia sighed when both men shook their heads. "Does your familiar?"

"Sami!" Jag turned as Sami slipped into the room through the pocket between realms. His ears lifted expectantly. "Can you pick a lock?"

"No, Master."

"Dammit." Jag pointed at the case. "Can you use your ability to make portals to get into the case?"

Sami winced, wringing his fingers together. "I don't know, Master. Remember what I said the night before?"

"Yes. But this would only be moving it from inside the case to outside. Not travelling realms."

Sami made a low whine in his throat. "I suppose I could try." He inched towards the case and peeked inside, his ears lifting as he spied the book. Wiggling his clawed fingers, he hesitated only a moment before they disappeared into the air. Jag, Ethan, and Olivia leaned over the case, watching as Sami's disembodied fingers appeared like green little snakes beside the tome. Carefully, he inched his black claw forward and touched the corner of the page, jerking back quickly as if it was hot.

There was a long pause before Sami exhaled in relief. With a mouth full of tiny, needle teeth, Sami grinned at his master and gave him a thumbs up. Jag nodded in approval.

Sami reached his full hand into the case and grabbed the book —and immediately burst into a pile of nightmarish bugs from hell.

Ethan and Olivia screamed, stumbling backwards in terror as

black-shelled cockroaches, spindle-legged spiders, green scorpions, and slithering worms began skittering across the floor.

"Oh my God!" Olivia climbed onto a table to get away from the swarm, Ethan scrambling up beside her.

"Is Sami dead? What happened?!"

"Satan help me," Jag growled in annoyance. "Don't step on any. We need all of them for him to regenerate."

"Sami is made of *bugs*, Jag?" Ethan hissed as a roach crawled up the table. "Ah, Sami, stop it!"

"Of course he's made of bugs. What are your pets made of?" Jag shook his head, gathering piles of bugs with his big hands and piling them back together.

"Not bugs!" Olivia screamed. "Not gross, terrifying bugs!"

"What the hell is going on?" A new voice joined the chorus, standing at the entrance to the library. The older man wearing a maintenance shirt and jeans stormed inside, stopping short at seeing the mass of bugs all over the case.

"There's an infestation!" Olivia pointed at the case. "They're all over the books! We need to get them out! Right?" She elbowed Ethan, snapping him out of his haze.

"Oh—oh! Right! The books in that case are priceless. If the insects get to them, they'll be ruined. Do you have keys?"

"Good God!" The poor man's face went pale as he fumbled with his keys. "I need to go get some poison!"

"We'll get the books out. You grab the poison." Ethan gestured for the keys. "We'll need to get these out of the way if you're going to be dousing it with bug spray anyway."

The keys came soaring through the air in a lazy arc, and Ethan caught them with both hands.

"I'll be right back! Don't let those scorpions near you!" The maintenance worker tossed over his shoulder as he ran out of the room.

Jag carefully stepped around the swarm of bugs meandering around his feet and took the case key from Ethan. Once the case's lock sank back, Jag plucked the book out and handed it over to Olivia.

"Ethan. Help me gather up Sami." Jag made a pouch with his shirt, scooping bugs off the ground and dropping them into place.

"Me? Why me?" Ethan shuddered. "Aren't they deadly?"

"He won't attack you. Olivia I'm not sure about, but I know he won't attack you. Quickly, before the human with the poison comes back and I have to kill him."

"Ew, ew, ew..." Ethan eased off the table, trying to summon the courage to grab at the creepy crawlies darting around their shoes. One would think that plucking up scorpions, spiders, and other grotesque little monsters would get easier after the first few, but that was a damn lie. Each bug behaved differently, and Ethan couldn't hold back the low-pitched whine that bled from his throat each time he had to touch one.

Book in hand and bugs in shirt, the trio escaped the library before the maintenance worker could come back for a daring rescue. The leathery binding of the book felt wonderful in Ethan's hands, the solution to their problems finally at his fingertips. Now Ethan could fix the tears, undo the bubbling apocalypse, and maybe even touch his boyfriend again.

"I'm so glad this is almost over." Ethan hugged the book to his chest, his stomach finally easing after days of stress. "Once we get home, we can find the missing passage and get this settled."

"Yes." Jag nodded, the bug-filled pouch against his stomach squirming around as he held it closed. "We can put this behind us. I told you we'd solve this, Ethan."

"Yeah." Ethan smiled, feeling lighter than he had in a long time. "You did. And it'll be good to be able to continue my research too." He unlocked the car and placed the book gently inside of a travel-sized suitcase lined with old sweaters. Ethan made sure to secure the book in place, wrap it up, zip the case shut, and slide it into the backseat. Nothing was going to touch that book until they got home where it was safe.

Ethan took a deep breath, the first one he'd had since the frogs rained from the sky. Cool, late morning air blew his hair. The cloudless sky was bright blue and promised a sunny day. Taking the moment as a victory, Ethan leaned over to Jag and dared to plant an innocent kiss on his cheek.

The demon smirked, and Ethan's heart fluttered just a little.

No clouds formed; no thunder rolled overhead. Ethan felt like he had conquered hell itself by braving the university, saving the book, and wrangling a swarm of bugs.

Everything was going to be okay.

The rumble under their feet made some car alarms in the parking lot go off, and Olivia grabbed Ethan's shoulder for balance.

"Are we having an earthquake?" She stumbled and nearly pitched forward, and Ethan almost followed her down. The cement under their feet cracked and groaned, the ground shifting and rolling dramatically. The earth under Ethan's car parted, the machine tilting to the side as a massive, impossibly large creature emerged. Veiny, pale flesh stretched over an eyeless skull the size of a tank pushed up from the depths of the planet, its wide maw a spinning, pulsing wall of muscle and teeth yawning up towards the sky. With a silent scream, the wormy nightmare sank its teeth into Ethan's car and curled into itself, wrapping the crushed metal sedan with its large, fleshly body and unforgiving mouth.

As quickly as it had emerged, it was gone, sliding back into the gaping hole caused by its presence.

The ground slowly calmed. The rumbling stopped. The car alarms and oblivious birds singing was the soundtrack of the frozen reality they stood in. Olivia gripped Ethan's arm in silence, mouth hanging open in horror. Jag sighed, his shirt still squirming with bugs.

Everything was not okay.

11

ALWAYS TIP

The human that was summoned to take them home was not pleased by Sami's condition.

Angry stares and mutterings from a disgruntled servant was the least of Jag's concerns. The book was lost, Ethan was upset, and Jag's familiar was in pieces. Ethan had mentioned that he made sure to tip really well, but Jag hadn't seen any charms exchanged.

Olivia procured a large glass tank they could deposit Sami's parts in while he attempted to heal, the container apparently a relic from when Ethan had a large lizard named Larry. Apparently, it had grown to enormous proportions and escaped, bolting out of the back door into the wild while Ethan was cleaning its tank.

"What the hell do we do now?" Ethan flopped on the couch, placing his head in his hands. "The book and my *car* are gone. I don't think insurance covers giant nightmare worms, so I'm pretty screwed."

"You can borrow my car whenever you need it, Ethan." Olivia sat next to him, rubbing his back. "We'll figure it out."

"What about the book?" Ethan dropped his hands away,

looking at her before swinging his gaze to Jag. "We don't exactly have a Plan B."

Jag wasn't used to feeling helpless. It wasn't an emotion he liked, so much so that it made him physically cringe. Most of his problems throughout his life could be solved with killing something and calling it a day. Being reliant on magic he hated and didn't understand was sour and bitter in the back of his throat, and he felt weak for not being able to keep Ethan from looking so desperately defeated.

"I don't know, Ethan." Jag swallowed the bad taste in his mouth. "But we haven't lost yet. If I've learned anything about magic, it's slippery but plays by a firm set of rules. There is a way to defeat it—we just need to figure out how."

"How can we know the rules if the guide was swallowed up by a worm?" Ethan shook his head. "I'm not helping, I know. I just don't know what to do."

Olivia nodded towards the glass tank. "You said Sami is...coming back to life, right?"

"Yes." Jag peered into the tank. "The bugs are already starting to fuse together and tether. He'll be back to normal soon."

"Great," she said around a gag. "Maybe we should call it a day, let Sami heal. We can tackle this tomorrow. I think today has been tough on all of us." She gave the tank a weary look. "Some more than others."

"Yeah." Ethan rubbed his forehead with his fingers. "I guess we can't fix this today."

Olivia wrapped Ethan in a hug and held him close, and Jag felt a pang of jealousy in that embrace. He would have gladly severed a limb to be able to comfort Ethan properly. Instead, he had to keep his distance, or something horrible might gulp down a piece of Ethan's house.

"You two get some rest." Olivia stood. "I need to go process this day and maybe do my own research. And by research, I mean drink a lot and play with my tarot cards."

"Thanks, Olivia." Ethan gave her a weak smile.

Jag managed a nod of appreciation as she passed, and she gave Sami's tank a friendly tap on her way out. The room fell into a silence as Ethan stared at the floor, his eyes vacant as his mind retreated back into itself.

"Ethan." Jag sat on the couch, giving him a cushion of distance. "I'm sorry the worm ate your car."

"It's my fault." He rubbed at his eyes with his fingers. "I got cocky and gave you a kiss. What was I thinking?"

"If it helps, I was going to do the same." Jag shrugged. "You acted faster than I did. But that kiss was inevitable."

The small chuckle that Ethan let slip was a victory. "That does make me feel better."

Jag fought the urge to reach across the couch and touch him. Instead, he ran his palms over his jeans and cleared his throat. "Perhaps we can still salvage this day."

"How could we possibly do that?" Ethan leaned back into the couch, his head resting against the cushions. "Other than get really drunk and go to bed at like three in the afternoon?"

"We haven't begun to prepare the house for Hallow's Eve." Jag motioned to the decorations still resting in plastic bags. "I can assist. There is cotton to spread over walls and fog to summon. And you bought gourds for us to carve, correct?"

"Pumpkins, yeah." Ethan's laugh was still weak, a ghost of the bright sound Jag had grown to adore. Ethan ran his hands down his face, his head still tilted backwards. "I don't know if I'm in the Halloween spirit right now, Jag."

Jag felt the pull to comfort him again, the feeling so powerful it trampled over his sense of pride. The spell Ethan had on him was intense, a bone-deep grip that took hold of his marrow and pushed him to his feet. The treasure he was after was in the second bag, having been tossed inside in a hurry after a flaming fish crashed onto the hood of a now-eaten car.

Jag slipped the devil headband on and turned to Ethan. "How about now?"

"Oh my God."

"You praise Satan when you're around a demon, human." Jag motioned to the fabric horns. "And this demon demands you prepare for the Devil's Holiday."

"If I called you cute right now—"

"I am mighty and evil," Jag corrected before he could finish. "The blood of my fallen enemies polishes the blade of my sword, their entrails fed to the black buzzards and skulls pierced on my banner." The headband slipped forward so he pushed it back in place. "I am not *cute.*"

Ethan's face split into a grin, a real one that dimpled one cheek. "Right. Of course."

"On your feet, mortal." Jag tossed a bag of cotton webbing at him. "We have children to terrify."

The afternoon was spent toying with an electronic spider with the wrong number of eyes, spreading cotton webbing over bricks, stringing lights up over the doorway, and watching Ethan summon fog to "test" the machine. Jag offered to bring Ethan more skulls to add around the foam gravestones in the yard, but Ethan assured him it wasn't necessary. A large skull right at the center would have been perfect, but his suggestion was denied.

The pumpkins were disgusting and glorious. Inside the large orange gourds was a stringy mess covered in seeds. The sticky carnage felt familiar as Jag squished it between his fingers. He couldn't understand why Ethan wasn't more enthralled by it. Apparently, the seeds were often cleaned and baked as a luxury food item, and Jag was excited to try it.

Even though Jag had spent centuries honing his skills with a blade, his ability to make anything resembling a face in the pumpkin was drastically lacking. Jag's pumpkin looked deformed and perhaps constipated, the eyes a bit too close together and the mouth a total disaster. Ethan, on the other hand, was an artist, his pumpkin a grinning face with jagged teeth and narrow, haunting eyes. The flush around Ethan's neck and ears was telling that he wasn't expecting Jag's praise.

When the sun was low enough, Jag was able to see the brilliance of their work so far.

The lights flickered green and orange, the synthetic fog rolled across the skull-less grass and gravestones, and their pumpkins of various skill levels greeted them with candlelit smiles. The spider wiggled at them when they approached the front door, and Ethan jumped even though he had placed it there.

"Not bad." Ethan smirked at his yard. "We can still add a couple things, but this isn't bad at all."

"I think this might scare some children." Jag nodded, having no idea if human children would be scared of their work. Maybe they would be uncomfortable with his pumpkin, but anyone with eyes would be.

"I'm going to go shower. Then I'll roast those pumpkin seeds."

Jag watched Ethan start climbing the steps towards the bedroom. "I wish I could join you."

He smirked over his shoulder. "Me too." Ethan paused on the steps. "It's only been a couple days. I didn't think it would be this hard. What are we going to do if we can't fix this, Jag? What if we can never touch each other again?"

The thought of that made Jag's sternum fold into his heart, a block of lead filling his stomach.

"That won't happen."

"I really hope you're right." Ethan sighed, his shoulder slumping as he finished the climb upstairs. Jag's chest had a sharp pinch as he retreated away from the stairs, taking solace in the dark living room.

Inside the glass tank, Sami was sitting upright, rubbing his eyes. Most of his bugs had fused and reformed his small shape. Only a couple stragglers were still finding their way to one long ear.

"Greetings, Master," Sami said around a yawn.

"You seem to be almost back together." Jag gave him a onceover. "I thought it would take longer."

"I hope it wasn't too much of an inconvenience, Master." His almost-formed ears lifted. "Did you get the book?"

"Almost. We ran into a complication." Jag scowled. "A razor-maw worm complication. Ethan's car and the book have been lost."

His ears dropped. "Oh."

Jag grunted, his will to continue the conversation fading. Exhaustion was starting to set in, as was the persistent buzz of longing from his absence from Ethan. A tiny, malicious tapping was starting to strike in the back of his head, that perhaps he might never feel Ethan's skin ever again. Never hold him in his arms. It made Jag want to rip something in half and maybe cry.

Except demons didn't cry. So he'd have to settle for tearing something in half and maybe yelling.

While wallowing in his grief, the fragile veil between realms warbled and rippled in the middle of the living room. It was similar to Sami's entrance, the air bending and moving in a way that was unnatural to the human world. Instead of a small, fidgety familiar bringing news or supplies, something else entirely emerged.

Jag had only ever seen Messengers a handful of times in his long existence, and he knew from experience they never carried good news. Like familiars, these creatures were constructed from magic to serve, and did so without fail.

The towering figure of bone and determination hunched their shoulders to stand in the room, long antlers of black and gold scraping against the popcorn ceiling. Robes of black rags hung off their frame, a couple bells and charms rattling around a permit that was pinned securely in place.

A fleshless face tilted towards Jag, jaw opening in greeting as their spindly fingers uncurled like a spider. The sealed letter inside was stamped with his clan's blood seal. Normally the sight of that stamp would ignite the fire of war in Jag, spurring on a happy bellow of bloodlust while he ran to fetch his battle-won armor.

Now it made him feel sick. Very sick. His stomach was filled with sharp stones and acid.

The letter was plucked from the Messenger's hand, and Jag motioned for them to wait a moment. The skeletal creature froze in place, waiting patiently as Jag retreated to the kitchen and pulled a magnet in the shape of a piece of fruit from the refrigerator. He placed it in the boney palm of the creature, who inspected it with hollow eye sockets. Between two long fingers, the tiny plastic strawberry was plucked up and attached to one of the bells, the offering accepted.

Dipping their antlers, the Messenger passed back through the void without a trace.

Sami shifted in the glass tank, sitting up to peer over at the letter. Jag stared at the seal longer than he should, before finally popping it open.

"We're going to war." Jag's voice sounded distant to himself, like someone else was speaking. "The dark prophecy has come to pass."

"You mean..." Sami swallowed. "*The* dark prophecy? The Retaking?"

"Yes." Jag set his jaw and crumpled the letter in his fist. "The demons have formed an alliance. They're coming for the humans."

"W-when, Master?"

Jag let his palm heat with his rage, the paper bursting into flames before falling to wisps of ash on the floor.

"Hallow's Eve."

12

GET BEHIND ME, DEMON

After a long, crappy night of sleep, Olivia arrived early with donuts and coffee. Ethan had once again slept alone in his bed, Jag slumbering on the couch to keep them from accidentally touching. The bad night of sleep soured Jag's mood, and he barely spoke while they devoured sugary breakfast and caffeine. Even with a mouthful of sprinkle donut, Jag held his scowl.

Sami was all better and no longer a pile of squirming, nightmare bugs. The little green goblin happily ate an entire bag of donut holes while perched on the kitchen counter.

"Okay, so." Olivia rubbed her hands together. "After a full night of alcohol and witchy research, I have some ideas. Well, I have more questions than ideas, but still a good lead."

"At this point, anything is good." Ethan picked pieces off of his half-eaten blueberry cake donut.

"Would you be willing to walk me through the night you summoned Jag? What you did, where you were, words spoken, all of that? I want to walk through it like we're reconstructing a crime scene."

"Okay." Ethan eyed his friend with growing apprehension. Equating the summoning to a crime scene made his stomach hurt. "Like I said, anything is good at this point. But...why, exactly?"

"Clues, Watson," she said around the last bite of her jelly donut. "In fact, why don't we set everything up like you had it that night? Maybe not exactly so we don't have a repeat." She tilted her head in Jag's direction, then paused and lifted a brow. "Unless maybe you have any friends who are into human women?"

Jag didn't seem to hear her, glaring at the donut box like he was trying to set it on fire with his mind.

"Jag?"

The demon's attention snapped back, his eyes lifting to bounce between them. "What?"

"Are you okay?" Ethan almost reached out to touch his hand but stopped himself. "You're a little distracted today."

"Yes. I'm fine." He took another bite of his food. "What were you asking me?"

"Olivia was asking if you had friends who would perhaps want to mate with her," Sami chimed in from the counter.

"*Mate?*" Olivia nearly choked on her coffee. "Not mate. Just you know..." She shimmied her shoulders a bit. "Have some fun. Do you had any bi demon boys or sultry lesbian lady demons you could hook me up with?"

"I do, but they might kill you in the process."

Olivia nodded in consideration. "Okay."

"Focus, please." Ethan rubbed his tired eyes. "We can get Olivia murder-laid later."

"I'm going to grab your notebook and laptop. You said you summoned him in the basement, right?" The last bits of jelly were licked from Olivia's thumb as she got to her feet. Ethan nodded in answer to her question, and she disappeared to fetch the items needed for the crime scene reconstruction.

"You sure you're okay, Jag?" Ethan whispered once Olivia was gone. "You seem off today."

"I have a lot on my mind." Jag exhaled through his nose, his gaze drifting from his plate to Ethan's. "You should try and eat more, Ethan."

"I'm not that hungry this morning. Do you want my half?" Ethan slid his plate over towards him. "Maybe it'll help energize you this morning."

Jag stared at the picked-apart donut, his face in a state of blank sorrow that Ethan couldn't quite read. For a mighty champion and all-around badass, Jag seemed deflated, tired, and maybe a little sad. Before Ethan could ask if something was wrong, Jag's shoulders squared, and he stood from the table.

"Come. Let's go assist the witch."

"Sure..." Ethan hedged, unsure what just transpired behind Jag's eyes.

Olivia was already in the basement with Ethan's laptop and notes, clearing some old boxes and the Christmas decorations out of the way so they had room for the crime scene. Having an audience while Ethan set up a very personal and embarrassing lack in judgement didn't help his stomach feel any better, but he concentrated on going through the motions for the sake of circumventing the apocalypse.

The summoning circle was easy enough to remember, a basic circle inside of a bigger one, outlined with specific symbols used to invoke the dark powers. It felt a little like being a kid playing with sidewalk chalk with the adult watching silently as he did his best attempt at art.

Ethan sat back on his heels and dusted his hands free of powder. "This is what I drew based on the outline in the book."

Olivia tapped one finger against her lips, studying the circle. "You just drew this, then read from the book? No candles or offerings?"

An uncomfortable wave of cold worms flooded his gut. "Um. Not an offering, really. From my research with the book, a lot of the incantations mentioned the need for a link or physical embodiment of those not present. I surmised that I probably needed something of David's here in order for it to...you know. Stick."

Olivia lifted her brows. "Oh, shit. Were you trying to curse him?"

"What? No! No." Ethan shook his head quickly. "Not curse. I don't want anything bad to happen to anyone." He quickly got to his feet and dug through some old boxes, lifting out the final piece of the summoning ritual. "I used his old sweater."

He didn't dare look, but he could feel Jag's eyes on him like hot beams on his back. Ethan quietly placed the folded garment in the center and continued. "After that, I drank a little wine and read the translation out loud. That's when Jag showed up."

Olivia leaned over to peer at the circle. "Did you smudge or smear any of the lines before you began?"

"No. Not that I remember."

"Candles?" She glanced his way as he shook his head. "And these symbols are exactly like the book?"

"Yeah, I copied them exactly."

"This is wrong." Sami crouched near the edge of the circle, pointing his long claw at one of the symbols. "It's backwards."

"What? Really?" Ethan leaned over to peer at what Sami was pointing to before grabbing his laptop. "I copied it directly from the book. It can't be backwards."

Sami's round, void-like eyes blinked at him as Ethan kneeled down beside the circle, comparing the two symbols. Staring back from the digital screen was the blood-inked script and drawings of the oath in all of its glory, thousands of years of ancient occult secrets buried within the unknown text of a demonic language. Ethan had spent months of his life poring over the symbols, memorizing each one in such vivid detail that he could recite them from memory.

And he wrote it backwards.

"Oh. I guess it is backwards." Ethan shrugged. "Whoops."

"Um." Olivia lifted both hands in outrage. "Did you just say 'whoops' about getting a symbol in a demonic summoning circle backwards?"

"Is...that bad?"

"Oh, honey." Oliva hung her head. "I've failed you as your witchy friend."

"It's bad," Sami confirmed. "This symbol backwards changes the meaning." He pointed out each symbol in order from the top, going counterclockwise. "Each of these symbols form the oath, the rules it goes by, and how the magic is to behave. You basically instructed it here to connect the magical flow between realms instead of binding Master to this world." Sami lifted one finger on each hand, drifting them away from each other as he said, "The tether is still open."

"Hence the tears." Olivia winced. "That's where it all went wrong."

"Not just that." Sami wasn't done dismantling Ethan's handiwork. "You were half right about the offering needing to be something connected to the person you're trying to curse."

"I wasn't trying to curse him!" Ethan shrugged his shoulders up in defense.

Sami ignored his outburst. "But this garment is not strong enough." He poked David's old sweater with his claw. "It needs to be a piece of that person's body. Hair. Teeth. Eyeballs. Blood. Fluid. Just a piece."

Ethan gagged. "That's disgusting."

"It's magic," Sami agreed. "Its roots are very primal."

"Great. So, I completely botched this, is what you're saying?" Ethan rubbed his temples as Sami nodded quickly.

"Completely."

"Great." Ethan adjusted to sit on his backside, tossing the chalk aside. "I'm dyslexic in Demon and failed to create a proper summoning circle because I'm not a psychopath who keeps hair and teeth around. What do we do now?"

"Well." Sami wrung his hands together, his ears lifting slightly. "We can re-do the curse—Oath." He slid his eyes over to Ethan as he sighed deeply. "By reconstructing the circle and completing the correct incantation. But we would still need a piece of him." He poked the sweater again. "For it to work."

"So we're back to square one then." Ethan rested his elbows on his knees and dropped his head forward.

"Not exactly." Olivia swooped in. "He's invited to my Halloween party."

"Seriously?" Ethan looked up at her, offended more than he had a right to be. "You invited my ex to your party?"

To her credit, Olivia seemed to absorb the look Ethan was throwing her way and toss it back in his face. "Well, I didn't want to make it awkward, Ethan, but he's kinda dating Ivan."

"Your cousin is dating my ex." It wasn't a question, but a flat sentence Ethan wanted to hang in the air.

"Why do you care who he's dating, Ethan?" She crossed her arms. "They make a cute couple."

"I don't care." Ethan dared to dart a look toward Jag, who was glaring at the backwards summoning circle. "I just wasn't expecting it."

"What I'm saying is that David is going to be at the party. We can grab a piece of his hair there and finish the spell." She shrugged.

When Jag finally spoke, his voice was low and hollow. "Is your party on Hallow's Eve?"

"No, it's two days before. Halloween is on a Monday this year, so we're having it the Saturday beforehand. Why?"

Jag shook his head. "Good. We'll get what we need there and finish the spell." He turned and went back up the stairs, leaving the basement quiet and a little cold.

Ethan felt a fist of icy lead coil in his stomach, and the droopy ears of Sami didn't help him feel better.

"I think you need to go talk to your boyfriend, Ethan. I'm going to head out." Olivia offered her hand down to help him up.

"Thanks, Olivia. Sorry for..." He trailed off as she waved it away.

"Call me later if you guys need a ride."

Ethan followed her back upstairs, waving goodbye as she left through the front door. Jag was in the kitchen, his gaze miles away as he scowled at the slightly dented box of donuts. A tiny whisper of doubt prodded him to go hide, leave Jag alone and let him ruminate over the conversation. Adding anything more to the topic would be a terrible idea, the verbal straw that broke the demon's back.

In that moment of silence in the kitchen, the situation was a classic example of Schrodinger's cat, both totally fine and a complete and utter disaster. Ethan wasn't sure if he could handle the latter.

"Hey." Ethan felt the urge to rub at his forearm, nerves prickling his spine.

"Do you love that human David?" Jag went in for the verbal gut punch, which Ethan should have been expecting. The question knocked the wind out of him just the same, and he had to inhale deep to answer.

"I did. Yeah." The forearm rub wasn't helping soothe his nerves. "I was with him for a long time."

"Did?" Jag's human eyes pierced through Ethan's heart like an amber arrow.

"I don't anymore. I think..." Ethan steadied himself with another long breath. "I think maybe I didn't for a while, even before we broke up. We drifted apart. I could tell it was happening, but the breakup still hurt. I think...maybe I was angry. Not at him." The shameful stinging in his eyes made him swallow. "At myself. For failing."

"Failing what?" Jag's voice seemed calmer now, but Ethan couldn't lift his eyes just yet.

"The relationship? I dunno. I just felt like I failed." Ethan cleared his throat and pretended to rub at his nose to dash a tear away. "I'm not the same guy I was nine months ago. I was in a really bad place. I don't want to be with David anymore, and I'm really sorry if I made you feel otherwise."

It was quiet for a long time, long enough that Ethan was finally baited to look up to meet Jag's eyes.

"You never need to apologize to me, Ethan."

"If I make you feel bad, I do. Or if I hurt your feelings because I'm being an asshole about an ex-boyfriend in front of you. I absolutely have to apologize for that."

Jag crossed his arms over his chest, dipping his chin. "I'll allow it under these circumstances."

"Thanks." Ethan felt a little ease in his stomach. "Are...we okay?"

"What do you mean?" Jag's dark brows creased.

"Us?" Ethan motioned between them. "Are we okay?"

Jag stared at him a long moment before straightening himself. "Ethan. Did you think something like this would drive me away?"

"I don't know."

"The only way I would leave your side is if you told me directly to do so," Jag stated so matter-of-factly that Ethan almost melted onto the floor. "If you do not love this human David, then he is no threat to me. You give me the word, and I will bring you mountains of skulls and flowers to prove that to you."

"We talked about the skulls," Ethan managed between feeling like his heart was about to burst. Jag moved across the kitchen, placing a hand on either side of Ethan so he was caged against the counter. The looming demon took great care not to touch his human captive as he leaned in close.

"I wish I could prove to you how devoted I am," he purred. "I'm tempted to let the worlds burn just to taste you again."

"Wow," Ethan breathed. "I'm very close to agreeing." The radiating heat of Jag's skin was a warm glow against Ethan, the proximity just close enough to tease but not indulge.

"Would you let the realms collapse to feel my tongues on you again, Ethan?" The heat tickling Ethan's skin made him shiver, Jag's lips frighteningly close to making contact with his neck. Spicy notes of Jag's body wash mixed with the musk of his skin washed over Ethan as the demon drew closer, his shoulders flexing as he kept Ethan in place.

"You're...being a very cliché demon right now." Ethan swallowed. "You do the temptation bit really well."

Leaning into the persona, Jag chuckled in his throat like he was born to play the role of the alluring dark spirit charming a helpless victim.

"Watching you trying to resist me is almost as fun." Jag pulled his mouth into a shark grin, full of threatening intentions and white teeth. "I could become addicted to this."

Ethan felt his body heating from the inside out from the idea that surfaced in his mind. "Do you...want to...watch me?"

The dark pupils in Jag's amber eyes flared wide, his voice straining to remain human. "Yes."

"Does that mean I can..." Ethan cleared his throat, trying desperately to sound sexy and not like he was vibrating with excitement. "Watch you?"

"Ethan. You are close to making me cause the end of the world." Jag pushed away from the counter. "To the bedroom, Ethan. Hurry." He swallowed. "*Please.*"

There was something intoxicatingly powerful about having a demon ask politely for something, especially when the object of his desire was one's body. Jag was the Champion of the Blood Wars, the one who wore his clan's armor.

And he just asked Ethan "please."

Ethan did as Jag asked, only he did so at a casual pace. Jag growled and followed along behind him, unable to do anything to speed the process along. Normally, halfway up the stairs, Jag would have swung Ethan over his shoulder and carried him, or they'd end up in various positions right on the stairs themselves.

But Jag was currently at Ethan's mercy. And it was kinda glorious.

"Patience, Jag," Ethan teased over his shoulder. "I can hear you growling."

"You're enjoying this." Jag narrowed his eyes as Ethan tossed him a cheeky wink.

"Little bit."

"You are playing a dangerous game, Ethan," Jag warned in a low rumble, following close behind as they finally entered the bedroom. "You might cause the end of the world."

"I think you can handle yourself better than that, Jagmarith." Ethan hesitated a moment, unsure how the next move would play out. "Strip and lose the charm. I want you naked and all demon."

When Jag stepped forward to glare down at Ethan, the playful smirk tugging the corner of his mouth took away any heat from his words.

"You dare command me, human?"

"I don't believe you have any choice, demon." Ethan bit his lip with a smile. "You're at my mercy. Now, do as I command."

Jag snarled his lip, stepping back to reach behind his back and tug his shirt off. There was no striptease when it came to Jag removing clothing, but he did love to do a slow reveal for his demon form. Twisting the charm between his fingers, Jag's skin shimmered between human and demon, his eyes flashing from amber to molten magma. His pants were discarded, the boxers following along with them, and soon, an otherworldly dream was standing naked in front of his bossy human boyfriend.

Jag looped the charm over his head, breaking the spell that made him seem human. His tan skin was replaced with his deep, crimson red hue, black horns curling up and out of his skull in their proud twist, his form growing inches taller and wider. Two churning firestorms watched Ethan, dark brows furrowing as he flexed his jaw to accommodate his very talented tongues.

During the nine months they had been together, Ethan had seen Jag shift into his demon form countless times. Somehow, even though Ethan knew what was coming and what to expect, it still took his damn breath away. Jag was impossible, unreal, an evil wet dream incarnate that Ethan got to touch and taste whenever he wanted.

"I'll never get sick of this," Ethan mumbled to himself, gazing over Jag's impressive and deliciously sinful body. Thick muscles, black hair trailing down his navel, proud and intense cock standing upright for attention.

And the tongues. Damn the tongues.

"I won't beg," Jag growled. "Don't keep me waiting. I want to see you."

"You're not giving the orders, demon." Ethan wagged his finger, then motioned to the bed. "Lay down."

The demon obeyed with a snarl, crawling onto the bed and leaning back against the charred headboard. His fiery stare burned Ethan as he made his way to the bed, slowly peeling off his clothing. The contrast between them was almost humorous. Jag was a pillar of strength and might, a mighty demon warrior with the body of an Olympian deity coated in the color scheme of a biblical boogeyman.

Ethan was very much none of those things. He was average, much smaller compared to Jag, and could easily be lost in a crowd. Yet the demon in his bed watched him like he was dipped in candy, his jaw flexing as Ethan shucked his pants and stepped out of them.

"Are you going to be able to keep your hands to yourself?" Ethan asked as he crawled onto the mattress, taking care to avoid bumping into him.

"No."

Ethan paused and lifted a brow. "Jag."

The growl that rumbled from him made Ethan laugh. Jag huffed out a bitter, "Yes."

"Good. Grab the lube."

Jag never removed his heated gaze from Ethan as he reached over and opened the bedside table, snatching the tube.

"Good, demon," Ethan purred, holding his hand out. Jag growled and dropped the plastic tube into Ethan's hand, watching with burning eyes as Ethan slowly uncapped it. Moving carefully, Ethan placed one knee on either side of Jag's left leg, taking care not to brush their skin together. The heat pouring from Jag's red skin warmed Ethan's thighs, causing him to shiver.

"Try not to move too much," Ethan ordered as he tilted the lube, dripping a line of slippery liquid down Jag's proud ridge. The demon hissed and jerked, watching Ethan with hungry eyes. "Give yourself a slow stroke."

Jag hummed in his chest, wrapping his fingers around his cock and squeezing, coating it with the slippery substance. The erotic sound of the lubricant slicking against his fingers caused a bloom of heat in Ethan, his own dick jerking in anticipation.

The cool drip of the liquid on his cock made Ethan groan, a stray drop landing on Jag's leg only to melt and evaporate.

"I could watch you for eons." Jag's horns scratched against the headboard as he tilted his head back, his hand slowly pumping. "You are more decadent than any delicacy I have ever had, more beautiful than a fallen battlefield, more sensual than any creature my home has to offer."

Ethan swallowed, bracing his hand on the burned wood beside Jag's horn. His fingers felt amazing, but it was Jag's eyes on him that was lighting the fuse. Jag's deep breaths filled his chest, expanding the expanse of crimson skin on display. Each slow pump was teasing and strong, his stomach tensing when he'd roam over the head. Ethan was hypnotized, moving his hand like Jag's to mimic what he must be feeling.

His thighs quivered when they fell in sync.

Even with the distance between them, their skin inches apart, Ethan could drown in the heat and musk glowing from Jag's body. Somehow, the demon was touching him without actually doing so, his presence tracing warm phantom tongues over Ethan's inner thighs. Ethan leaned down further, craving to feel more of the heat pouring from him, hissing when his hips, belly, and cock felt the waves of warmth from Jag.

"God, I can almost feel you," Ethan exhaled. "You're like the damn sun."

Jag inched closer, his breath a blast of summer wind against Ethan's ear. "Every inch of me burns for you, Ethan."

Pinpricks of sweat formed along Ethan's hairline, his body tight as a tingle of pleasure played down his spine. Jag's spicy scent, a musky blend of sweat and hellish delight, drifted over Ethan's like a dense fog of dreamlike ecstasy. Their fists moved at the same pace, slowly increasing each time Ethan dared to dip in further towards Jag's skin. They were too close, too damn close to touching and sending the world into a nightmare.

One touch. One small touch. That's all Ethan wanted, and that's all it would take to rip reality into shreds. The danger caused his heart to thunder, his sense of self-preservation to falter, and his body to tighten like a bowstring.

Jag's lips were whispering something to him, his body on fire with heat. The sounds of Ethan's cries of pleasure sounded far away. All there was in that moment was heat, Jag's skin, his smell, his voice, and the building wave about to break.

"I want to taste you." Jag's voice had slightly splintered, taking two different tones at the same time. His eyes seemed to pulse with a boiling glow, locked on the human straddling his thigh.

Before Ethan could respond or move, Jag's jaw flexed, his mouth opening to allow his long, sinful tongues to slither forth. Ethan gasped, thinking for a horrible, delicious moment that they were about to wrap around him like they normally did.

Instead, they crawled down to writhe near Ethan's cock, twitching and eagerly awaiting their prize.

Ethan felt the last bit of control snap, his body tensing as bolts of white-hot pleasure surged through his veins. The muscles in his shoulder shook as he held himself away from Jag. His thighs ached from the need to lean forward and run himself over the awaiting tongues. Watching himself spill over the twisting tongues of a panting, growling demon sent another blast toward him, and Ethan let his eyes flutter shut for a moment.

Jag's fist was moving quickly. His splintered voice roared in two different octaves as he cried out in pleasure, his head leaning back to gouge massive scars into Ethan's poor abused bedframe. Unlike Ethan, who had coated Jag's tongues in sticky evidence of his orgasm, Jag's cum was a totally new surprise.

"Jesus, Jag! Is your cum on fire?!" Ethan scrambled back as lines of flames painted Jag's panting chest, his churning eyes rolled back into his head. Jag flexed his jaw and restricted his tongues, smiling lazily as he coaxed out a couple more drops of flames from his cock.

"Yes."

"Why?!" Ethan jumped off the bed and tossed him a towel, yelping when the towel started smoking. Jag yawned and patted the flames out, using the now-charred towel to wipe himself clean.

"I had a lot built up."

"Does that always happen when you go a couple days?" Ethan watched warily from the bathroom door, using a different, not charred towel on himself.

"Usually, it's much worse."

"Jag." Ethan motioned to the smoking towel. "What if I had been giving you a blowjob?"

"That would have been much better than my hand. Your mouth is decadent."

Ethan chuckled, tossing the dirty and charred towels into the hamper before sitting down on the mattress. "I wish I could lay here with you like we normally do, but I guess it's too risky."

Jag sat up, the bedframe creaking with his shift in movement. Ethan watched as he pulled the sheet up from the bed, draping it between them just below Ethan's eyes. The feeling of Jag's lips against his, even with a cool piece of linen between them, made Ethan's heart flutter.

"I'll move back to the couch." Jag let the sheet drop, his volcanic eyes watching Ethan's. "We'll be back to normal soon, Ethan. I give you my word."

"I know." Ethan smiled, feeling a conflicting lightness in his chest even though his heart felt stubbornly heavy.

13

POWER TUNICS

"I wish I wasn't dreading this party so much." Ethan molded the treat made of popcorn and melted marshmallow into a ball. "I love Olivia's Halloween party more than her Christmas one."

"That is surprising." Jag was adding more green icing to his rotting corpse cookies, complete with graves made of crushed cookie dirt with candy worms. Ethan had found the idea on Pin-Interest, and Jag approved of the idea, though Jag's contribution of pink icing entrails was met with apprehension.

"The Halloween party is a little more loose and fun. People dress up in crazy costumes, and it's also not freezing cold outside." Ethan cracked a grin over his molding efforts. "No deadly snow yet."

"It was not pleasant, Ethan." Jag shot him a look before focusing back on his work.

Ethan let out a long sigh and checked on the jello-filled syringes in the fridge. "I really hope this ritual works."

"I have confidence that Olivia and Sami have worked out a decent plan." Jag wasn't *extremely* confident that a human witch and his familiar solved their problem, but he couldn't tell Ethan that. "We will adapt as the night progresses."

"That's what I'm worried about. I'd prefer it if we didn't have to adapt. I just want it to work so we can go back to our version of normal, which is being able to touch my demon boyfriend without causing monsters to burst from the ground and eat my car." Ethan leaned against the counter and crossed his arms, his shoulders shrugging up. "Is it bad that I'm almost more upset that we don't have a costume?"

Jag finished placing his last corpse into its cookie crumble grave and dusted off his hands. "Sami!"

"Yes, Master?" Sami slipped into view, holding two large plastic bags in his tiny, clawed hands. "Is it time? Now?"

"Yes."

Sami hopped up onto the dining room table and placed the bags down with a thump, grinning with needle teeth. "Everything you requested is here, Master." He tapped the bag on the right. "This one is Ethan's."

"Good. Begone." Jag waved him away, and Sami slipped away between realms. Jag lifted the bag Sami indicated was Ethan's and held it out for him.

"What is this?" Ethan carefully took the bag, obviously surprised by the weight.

"Your costume for tonight."

Ethan blinked, his face falling into an adorable shock. "You got me a costume?"

"Yes. I had Sami fetch it for us while we dealt with other things."

The splendors of Jag's home world had nothing over the brilliance of Ethan's full smile. Not even the great poisonous pits of his childhood could compare to the magnificence of the happiness painted over Ethan's face in that moment. A swell of pride filled Jag's chest, even more triumphant than when he slayed countless enemies on the field.

Maybe even more than when he was given his clan's armor.

The realization of that made him uneasy, but he was lost in watching Ethan tear open the plastic bag.

"Oh my God!" Ethan laughed, hefting the blue helmet from the bag. "You got me a Blue Ranger costume?"

"Yes. Sami informed me that the gloves should make sounds as well. It was difficult to find a size that fit us, but he finally found a version that worked."

Ethan giggled as he pulled the gloves on, fiddling with the back of his hands before chopping the air to hear the sound effect. The electronic noise that burst from it made him laugh and clap, sending more noise erupting from both hands.

"I haven't been a Blue Ranger since I was a kid! I can't believe you got me a—ah…" Ethan pulled the costume forward, scanning over it slowly. "Oh."

"They didn't have the version that had pants, but this tunic version was available."

"It's, um…it's a dress." Ethan blinked.

Jag opened his bag and lifted his helmet out. "I'll be going as a fellow Powerful Ranger warrior."

Ethan's laugh morphed into a snort, his hand making a boxy "swish" noise as he covered his mouth.

"You're the Green Ranger. Oh. My. God."

Jag puffed his chest out with pride. "Yes."

"Is your costume…yes, it is." Ethan's eyes widened as Jag held up his tunic.

"We will match."

"Jag. I…" Ethan shook his head in amazement, eying his costume and then Jag's. "I don't know what to say."

"This is our first Hallow's Eve together." Jag set his costume aside. "I wanted to make sure we were keeping with tradition, at least in some way."

Ethan smiled, a sweeter version of the bright star from before. "I love it. Thank you, Jag."

"I still do not understand how this is acceptable armor." Jag pulled the clothes he was wearing off, exchanging them with the warrior costume. "I do like that my legs are not constricted. But there is no metal plating or even thick leather to stop a blade." Jag smoothed the cloth down across his chest.

"I think in the show, they mostly dealt with lasers and magical blasts. Plus, most of their fighting was using their fists." Ethan was smiling as he watched Jag inspect his outfit. "It looks killer on you."

Jag didn't feel killer. He felt very confused. But he donned his helmet and helped pack up the treats for the party. Olivia arrived to gather them up for the party, having a similar reaction as Ethan did to the costumes. Her laughter bounced off the walls, and she demanded pictures before they could even leave the house.

Jag was unsure what was acceptable in the traditional garb, so he mimicked Ethan's poses, which were elaborate and strange. It was explained to him that standing with their fists outstretched and knees bent was a display of might and agility.

Humans were strange, small creatures. But Jag was charmed regardless.

"Do you have the laptop and your notes?" Olivia asked as she helped carry the trays of food out to her car. Ethan nodded and patted the laptop bag over his shoulder.

"All set."

"I got confirmation that David and Ivan will be at the party tonight. If they're not, I'm not above driving to their place and doing this the hard way." Olivia clicked her seatbelt into place. "But we'll see how it goes."

"One step at a time." Ethan sighed.

Showing up to Olivia's party in a Power Rangers dress was not the strangest thing Ethan had ever done, but it had cracked top five. After seeing the proud look on Jag's face when Ethan opened the bag, he didn't have the heart to tell him they weren't exactly "authentic." But Ethan also wasn't so insecure that he couldn't rock a "tunic" for a night, and Jag looked pretty cute in a Green Ranger dress.

Yet another thing Ethan had learned about himself while dating a demon. He liked a good dress on a man. Specifically, if it was a Green Ranger dress.

Since Olivia's house was spooky-themed year-round, she always went all out during her favorite holiday. Skeletons dressed as trick-or-treaters stood frozen in the yard, their boney hands outstretched with plastic pumpkin buckets filled with candy. Orange, purple, and green lights flickered in the tree around colored jars with electric tea lights inside, with a ghostly ghoul hanging low from the branches. Various yard signs featuring witches riding brooms, sparkly ghosts, and grinning pumpkins were planted in her actual pumpkin garden, which she had been growing.

She had even changed out her door mat to read "This Witch" and made sure the porch light was the proper spooky green color.

Inside, the house was overflowing with Halloween spirit.

A cauldron of punch was bubbling with dry ice, various treats shaped like chocolate spiders, marshmallow ghosts, and "poisoned" candied apples were out for guests. Jag's cookie zombies fit in very well in the buffet of creepy confections better than Ethan's popcorn balls.

The looming task of apocalyptic proportions seemed to fade into the periphery as Ethan took in the familiar delight of Olivia's yearly party. Music played low, various scary movies were playing on a projector outside, and the wood was ready to go for the firepit. A cauldron of punch was bubbling with dry ice. Various treats shaped like chocolate spiders, marshmallow ghosts, and "poisoned" candied apples were out for guests. Jag's cookie zombies fit in very well in the buffet of creepy confections, better than Ethan's popcorn balls.

It almost felt normal. It almost felt like Ethan was having a great Halloween, and the world wasn't on the brink of ending.

Guests started to trickle in, all donning their undead finest or their hysterical variety of pop-culture references. Ethan's dress was a big hit, and he was happy to pose with Jag, who was still obviously confused by the entire thing.

Mingling and catching up with friends helped ease Ethan further into the party, as did the crisp beer and amazing snacks. Jag stuck by for the most part, but Ethan's friends had adopted him into their circle over the past couple months. More often than not, Jag was munching on snacks talking about glorious battles he'd won.

No one believed him of course, but they thought he was damn funny.

Jag paused in his story to take a bite of a chocolate spider, tossing a glance towards Ethan. His smirk made Ethan grin like an idiot.

"Nice dress, Ethan."

David's voice felt like someone ripped the record needle away from his serene moment. His beer almost toppled. The plate of yummy critters lost two marshmallow ghosts and some zombie grave dirt.

"David. Hi. Hello." Ethan cleared his throat.

"Hello," David said slowly. "Didn't realize we were on formal terms now."

"Er—no! Sorry. I just wasn't expecting to see you again. I mean here! I didn't expect to see you *here*, at the party. Olivia's party." Ethan spun in a quick circle, desperate to put down his snacks and beer before he could spill more of it. He found a small table that barely fit both plastic dishes, having to push a tiny pumpkin onto the floor.

David's eyes were doing the wide stare of sardonic amusement, and Ethan remembered how much he hated that look. The silent judgment David would toss out with his facial expressions, like he had never been cringey or frazzled before.

Hell, who was Ethan kidding? David wasn't the frazzled type. The guy was always cool as a cucumber; it was one of the things Ethan had always liked about him. He had forgotten how much that look stung because Jag never did that to him.

As always, David looked great. Annoyingly, so did his new boyfriend. Both men were clearly gym rats, wearing midriff-baring costumes to accentuate the abs they sacrificed countless hours abstaining from carbs and fun to achieve.

"You remember Ivan?" David put his arm around Ivan's narrow waist.

"Yeah, of course. Nice to see you again, Ivan." Ethan reached his hand out for a greeting, and Ivan's grip was painful.

"So, you're like...a gender-swapped Power Ranger or something?" Ivan gave Ethan a pitiful onceover that was masked behind a smile. They were a dynamic duo of snobby facial expressions. Ethan felt like shrinking.

"Just a Power Ranger in a dress." Ethan shrugged. "Busting gender norms, am I right?"

"M'kay." Ivan gave David's chest a pat. "We're eighties aerobics instructors. Cute, right?"

"Super cute." Ethan motioned towards their attire. "You guys look great in...neon colors and headbands."

"David looks cute in everything," Ivan giggled, sneaking a kiss to David's cheek. "And nothing. But I don't have to tell you that."

"Ivan," David scolded with a laugh. "Behave."

Ethan tried not to vomit on their white sneakers.

"What? I can't help it. C'mon, lover. Let's go find something we can eat that's not soaked in sugar and fat." Ivan flashed another fake smile at Ethan. "Good to see you again, Ian."

"Ethan," he mumbled as they turned their well-toned backs and left. Olivia morphed into view at his side, dressed in her iconic felt witch's hat and black dress with silver spiderwebs accenting the sleeves.

"Did you get his hair?" she whispered, and Ethan hung his head.

"Damnit."

"We still have time." She handed him his beer and treats from the table. "You okay?"

"Was he always that shitty? That seemed meaner than normal. And no offense, Olivia, but your cousin is a douchecanoe."

Olivia snorted a laugh around her beer. "Honey, yes. David's kinda always been an asshole, but you're getting the full brunt now. And yeah, Ivan's a shit but he's just playing it up since you're the ex."

"Can you tell them to kindly fuck off then?" Ethan shoved a marshmallow ghost into his mouth.

"After we get his hair. Or you could sic Jag on them." She wiggled her eyebrows.

"I don't want them to be murdered," Ethan said around his ghost. "You don't know this, but Jag has a thing about collecting skulls."

"Fair enough." Olivia gave a halfhearted shrug, like maybe she didn't agree with Ethan's concern. "How about I rope them into a conversation, and you sneak up behind them and snag a piece of David's hair?"

"Um." Ethan felt queasy as Olivia handed him a tiny pair of scissors.

"I can hold them in a conversation. Just be sneaky."

"I really hate this."

"It'll be fine. He won't even notice." She finished her beer and set it aside. "Wait for me to start talking to them. I'll corner them over in the yard." Olivia gave him a wink and sauntered off with purpose. Ethan stared at the tiny scissors in his hand and swallowed the lump of dread in his throat.

You can do this, Ethan. He took a long breath. *You have to fix this. It's the only way to get the tears repaired. The only way you can be with Jag again.*

Ethan turned his attention back to where his boyfriend was learning how to play cornhole with other partygoers. Jag's dark brows were drawn down in concentration as he studied how people were tossing the small beanbag onto the board. When it was his turn, Jag cocked his arm back and hurled the small bag with force, sending it sailing into the middle hole and knocking the board backwards by about a foot.

Everyone stared in silence, except Jonathan, who was cheering and hooting. They apparently were playing teams.

Ethan felt a small burst of confidence as he tested the scissors out in his hand.

I can do this. For Jag.

True to her word, Olivia was able to wrangle David and her cousin into a conversation in the yard, close to the projector screen and a cooler of beer. Ivan stood with his arm lazily around David's waist, laughing at something Olivia was talking about. Every single footstep Ethan took sounded like he was stomping, his heartbeat flooding his ears as he slowly approached.

He tried to act casual, every so often pausing to pretend to stop and admire the yard or peer at the movie being played. At the third stop, Ethan tried to take out his phone, only to remember his dress didn't have pockets, so he felt around his body awkwardly before continuing.

Ethan's poor heart was trying to escape through his ribcage as he neared his mark. It was beating so terribly loud, there was a real concern his rapid-fire thumping would announce his presence.

David's shoulders were relaxed, arms crossed while he listened to Olivia chattering on and on about her latest office gossip. Ivan laughed and leaned into David a bit more. Ethan slithered in closer, fingers starting to shake.

Thank God David needed a haircut. His shaggy brown hair

wasn't cut tight to his skull like it normally was, and Ethan zeroed in on a small curl at the back of his head.

Careful.

Slow.

Hold your damn breath!

Ethan slowly reached up to snip the innocent curl from David's locks, the last piece to the puzzle to finally get everything back to normal—

SWOOSH

The electronic noise from Ethan's glove was like cannon fire, the digital sound effect of a punch flying betraying him. David ducked in alarm, spinning around. Ethan jerked his hands back sending both gloves into a round of sound effects as he dropped the scissors to the grass.

"What the hell, Ethan?" David scowled. "What are you doing?"

"Uh—ah—th-there was a bug! A big—" Ethan held up his hands to exaggerate the size of the fake insect. His gloves made swishing noises. "Huge bug! Like a beetle. I was trying to shoo it away."

"How about next time you just *tell* him instead of touching him without permission." Ivan's fake smile was long gone, his piercing eyes stabbing through the last bit of Ethan's confidence.

"Sorry. I'm really sorry." Ethan rubbed at his neck in embarrassment. "I should have asked."

"Yeah, no shit," David snapped. "Jesus, Ethan. I knew you'd be weird tonight, but this is kinda far."

"What?" Ethan shook his head. "I'm not being weird—"

"Hey, easy." Olivia stepped around them to stand with Ethan. "He was just trying to help. Let's just relax, okay? No drama at my party."

"Olly, your friend is being creepy and sad." Ivan crossed his arms.

"Ivan—" Olivia warned when another voice cut through the humiliating back and forth.

"What's going on?" Jag stood beside Ethan, his eyes dark as he scanned over Ivan and David.

Ivan spoke first, apparently not fearing the demon disguised as a human standing in front of him. "Your buddy here was trying to touch my boyfriend."

"Jag, this...this is David. And Ivan." Ethan gestured to each of them. "I was trying to get a bug out of David's hair." He looked at Jag to make sure he understood, but Jag's eyes were locked on the other men.

"Yeah, trying to get a bug from your ex's hair. Sure, man. I don't know what relationship you used to have, but he's—"

Jag snapped his eyes to Ivan. "Silence."

Ivan silenced.

Jag continued, moving his gaze back to David. "Ethan. You said there was a bug in his hair?"

"Um...yeah. A beetle or something." Ethan glanced between them as Jag took a step forward, grabbed a pinch of David's hair, and ripped out a small chunk. David yelped and grabbed his scalp in alarm.

"Got it," Jag said dryly. "It was a big one."

"The fuck, man?" David rubbed at his head. "Who even are you?"

"I am Jagmarith, second son of Bolor'gath, Champion of the Blood Wars and carrier of my clan's armor. I'm also Ethan's boyfriend, and tonight, I'm a Green Power Ranger as is custom for Hallow's Eve."

"...What?" David's face was a mess of confusion and anger. Ethan had to stifle a laugh as he followed Jag back to the snack table.

"That was amazing." Ethan smirked at him, holding his hand out for the clump of hair. Jag passed it to him, squeezing his hand around Ethan's since they were both wearing gloves. "Thanks for not killing him."

"I thought that I wasn't allowed to do that?"

"You're not. But I know you wanted to." Ethan gave his wrist a squeeze, and Jag grumbled.

"Do you have what you need for the ritual?"

"Yeah, I think so. I just need a place to draw out the circle, and we can read from the pages."

Olivia joined them by the table, exhaling in frustration as she ate a zombie cookie.

"I'm sorry they were being twats. You have the hair, right?"

"And probably a little scalp." Ethan winced. "Where can I do this where people won't interrupt?"

"Well, it's a Halloween party at my house," she explained around her snacking, shrugging. "So honestly, someone drawing a demon summoning circle wouldn't be the weirdest thing they've ever seen."

"I'd rather have a little privacy. What about your basement?"

"It's carpeted now, remember?" Olivia motioned for them to follow her as she made her way back inside. In a drawer filled with miscellaneous cords, coupons, and twist ties was a container of sidewalk chalk that had clearly been used before. "You can use this and draw on my driveway."

"In the front yard?" Ethan balked. "How is that private?"

"Better than back here. It'll be fine. All my neighbors are either in for the night or partying anyway. Plus, I draw weird shit on my driveway all the time. It's fine."

"Oh my God." Ethan took the chalk. "I hate this idea."

"I'll keep everyone in the backyard with a game." Olivia gave him a quick, tight hug. "Good luck!"

Ethan swallowed as Olivia scurried back outside to her party, leaving him and Jag standing in the kitchen with sidewalk chalk and a mission.

Fix the ritual.

Repair the tears.

Save the world.

No pressure.

14

THE RETAKING

"You look pale, Ethan." Jag held the open laptop in his hands while Ethan studied it, his forest-green eyes scanning the digital pages.

"I think my spiders and ghosts might come back up."

"You did this once before. There is no reason why it won't work a second time."

"I did it once before so incorrectly that the world is tearing itself apart," Ethan corrected, his eyes bouncing up to Jag. "What if I make it *worse*?"

"That is a possibility."

"Jag!"

"But we cannot leave things as they are now," Jag soothed as best he could. "I cannot live in a universe in which I cannot touch you every moment. It's either we fix the tears, or I'm going to eventually cause the end of days because you tempt me to disregard all sense of self-preservation just to feel your skin against mine."

The fear in Ethan's rich gaze melted into something else, but his skin didn't darken as much as Jag had hoped it would.

"What if it doesn't work, Jag? What do we do if it doesn't work?"

A tendril of cold wrapped itself around Jag's heart and squeezed. "It will, Ethan. We must try."

With a long exhale through his lips, Ethan gave a jerky nod and said nothing.

Jag stood still, allowing the human to study the computer screen before kneeling down and beginning to draw. The chalk in his hand left a pink mark behind as Ethan drew the summoning circle against the cement. The wind outside blew lazily, the soft bite of encroaching winter lingering on the skin. Across the street, a child on a bike whizzed past, barely giving them a glance.

Ethan carefully constructed the portal between the realms in chalk, popping up to gaze at the screen in order to get the symbols exact. It was grueling to wait, to watch Ethan take his precious time to be correct.

Jag's stomach was alive with buzzing nerves and doubt, but he wouldn't dare say it aloud.

"Okay. Does it look right?" Ethan dusted the chalk dust off his hands, smearing pink ghosts across his tunic.

Jag swiveled the laptop around, studying Ethan's circle and the one scanned from the book.

"Yes. It seems correct."

Ethan gave another small nod, his curls bouncing as he kneeled down again. Wrapped in an orange paper napkin with black spiderwebs, Ethan placed the clump of David's hair in the center of the circle and weighed it down with the chalk. He stood again and took his place beside Jag.

Jag didn't pressure Ethan to start, allowing him to take measured breaths and shut his eyes for a moment. With a gloved hand, he pressed his palm against Ethan's lower back in support. Ethan's breath seemed to come a little easier after that.

"Okay," Ethan breathed. "Here goes nothing."

Jag grounded his stance and stood still as Ethan began reading from the pages. The language was ancient and familiar, as if something Jag heard in a dream once before. Ethan's tongue tilted it in strange ways, the pronunciation correct but with a human hue to the words, coloring them in a strangely beautiful melody. The real language, Jag's ancestral language, wasn't built to accommodate human linguistic limitations. Yet this melding of the two was harmonious and surreal, like a pleasant fever dream.

Jag had been so lost in the cadence of Ethan's words he had barely noticed the passage had finished. Ethan stood stock-still, no breath leaving his body.

The wind jostled the napkin, flapping one corner. Jag felt his tunic press into the back of his legs, the cold nipping at his skin.

The child on their bike passed by again.

"What happens now?" Jag eventually asked in the stillness. "Is there another passage?"

"No," Ethan said around an exhale. "That's all of it." He stepped forward and glanced up and down the street, then winced up at the sky. "Did it work?"

"What happened last time you did this?"

"You showed up." Ethan laughed. "You just materialized into existence in my basement."

"Did you see anything before that?"

"No. It was just me and my basement." He shrugged. "Being lame and lonely."

Jag shut the laptop and set it on the hood of Olivia's car. "I suppose there is a way we can test it."

Ethan held his breath again as Jag stepped in close, tracing a gloved thumb across his cheek.

"What if we kiss and everything goes to hell again?"

"At this point." Jag leaned in, watching Ethan's eyes flutter closed. The sugary smell of chocolate spiders was still on his lips, and Jag felt so terribly hungry in that moment. "Let it."

Satan, had Jag been waiting for this moment. This longing

desire to feel Ethan's lips against his had nearly broken him, torn down his warrior resolve, and crushed his spirit.

But now he was his again. Finally.

Finally.

The sharp shriek of a child snapped Jag back from his haze just in time to see a child racing by on a bike in terror. Ethan blinked his eyes and turned towards the noise, glancing up at the swirling sky. The once pink-and-orange sunset was swallowed into a vortex of black-and-purple fog, the wind warming with the scent of sulfur and ash.

"Oh, God," Ethan whispered. "This looks bad."

"Master!" Sami stumbled from the air, his portal shimmering and swirling in the air. "Master, something has happened!"

"I'm aware," Jag snapped.

"Ethan!" Olivia's voice carried from the backyard. "Ethan, get over here now!"

"Shit!" Ethan darted back into the house, rushing towards the backyard.

"Sami, bring me my armor," Jag tossed over his shoulder as he chased after Ethan.

"Master—"

"Now, Familiar! Go!"

Jag didn't stay to watch if Sami disappeared, chasing Ethan through the house before staggering out into the backyard. Olivia's decorations were knocked down, chairs overturned, and snacks littered the grass. Suspended in the air, long scars torn between the fabric of their realities pulsed and jerked like angry red wounds. Something was pushing against them from the other side, their forms outlining the threadbare barrier.

"What the *fuck* is going on?" Olivia demanded, unable to take her eyes off the rips extending out into her Halloween oasis.

"Oh my *God*," Ethan huffed again, his hands covering his mouth in horror.

"What are those things?!" someone else demanded. Another

person screamed as the barrier began to rip, a clawed hand escaping through.

"Stand back!" Jag ordered, but the humans didn't budge, either too enthralled or horrified to do much more than stare.

"Jag!" Ethan called as Jag stomped towards the tear, ready to face whatever was about to spill forth. The tear with the hand widened and tore higher, threads of reality snapping and stretching like overstretched flesh. Birthed from the wound between earth and Jag's home, a demonic force ripped free with a chorus of bellows, clattering armor, and raised weapons.

Jag snarled at those who would threaten his territory, his home, and his humans.

The three demons that escaped through the tear saw his defiance and laughed in mocking delight.

"Look at this human!" Kurkoch of the Flayed pointed at Jag. He was a stocky brute, mostly gut and rage, and had won his clan's armor during the Battle of Bile's Pit. "He wants to challenge us!"

Gor'than, a pole of a demon with a bony back that curved inward like an overstretched bow, cackled. "Let him die screaming!"

Last and certainly not least, Bulgaz, the silent axe-wielder of the Splinterbone clan, scanned over Jag with piercing eyes. He did not share the boisterous attitude of his battle mates and watched the scene play out with obvious boredom.

"Jag…" Ethan called, his voice shaking with worry.

"Are you the best the humans have to offer?" Kurkoch scoffed as he hefted his large frame towards Jag. "Small, fleshy thing. He doesn't even have weapons."

"I need no weapons to defeat you, Kurkoch," Jag spat. "Your specialty is only your massive gut and the contents within. Not your warrior abilities."

"This flesh sack knows you, brother." Gor'than clattered his long teeth. "Your accomplishments have traveled beyond our realm!"

"You know of my victories, small human? You wish to worship me?" Kurkoch smirked, his meaty hands resting on his hips. "Go on. Bow before the mighty Kurkoch, and I will spare you."

Jag tilted his head back and laughed.

"How *dare* you!" Kurkoch swelled his cheeks with the acidic bile that championed his victory when Jag finally slipped his charm over his head.

The shift back to his demonic form stretched the tunic to its limits, but Jag was impressed the fabric held in his larger form. Some of the color from the green pattern splintered white from the strain, but the design was still present.

Kurkoch's tallow eyes widened, and he swallowed his weapon.

"J-Jagmarith!" Gor'than's back curled more. "What are you doing here?"

"As a human!" Kurkoch added.

Bulgaz seemed less bored.

"This is my realm." Jag beat his fist against his chest. "I wear the armor of the great human heroes. I fight for them now. If you trespass here, I will kill you all."

"You fight...*for* the humans?" Kurkoch nearly choked on his spit. "What in Satan's name are you talking about?"

"Betrayer!" Gor'than shouted, lifting his curved blade. "We claim this land for the Venomguts!"

Jag sighed in annoyance, grabbing Kurkoch by the horn and twisting him around to face his brother. With a swift punch to the side of Kurkoch's massive gut, an explosion of volcanic puke erupted from Kurkoch's gullet, splashing over the curved form of the annoying and pointless Gor'than.

A shrill scream burst from the melting demon, his armor falling away as his flesh pooled around him in a heap. Only his fragmented, crooked skeleton remained.

Bulgaz laughed, pulling his axe from the holster on his back. "You spilled first blood, Jagmarith of Clan Worm. Now we get to pull you apart at the seams."

"We will feed your bones to the soul ravens! These humans will feel my bile on their—" Kurkoch made a choking whimper as Jag twisted his horns quickly, snapping his neck. His body fell into a rolling heap, and Jag rolled his shoulders back.

"It's Clan Montgomery, Splinterbone. I am Jagmarith, second son of Bolor'gath, Champion of the Blood Wars, and carrier of the armor of the Green Ranger. The human realm is mine."

Behind Bulgaz, the pulsing wound between the realms tore higher, the barrier stretching as more of Jag's world tried to burst into Olivia's backyard.

"You have me and all seven clans to deal with, Jagmarith. The Retaking is at hand." Bulgaz flipped his axe in his hand. "I will see you fall and take your precious humans for myself."

"Master! Sword!" Sami slipped from his portal, holding out Jag's blade just as Bulgaz charged forward to swing. Somewhere behind him, Ethan cried out in alarm, and Jag brought his onyx blade up to deflect Bulgaz's crimson axe.

"Help Ethan close the tear, Sami!" Jag ordered, stepping back from the force of the blow. "More are coming!"

Screams of the party guests filled the backyard as a crack of thunder erupted from the sky, the swirling clouds darkening as the tears bulged. Small fissures in the rift allowed leaks through. Firehornets and fleshrotter beetles started skittering across the grass. Olivia smashed one with her heeled boot. A hornet got knocked from the sky by a plastic Halloween bucket.

Bulgaz's swings were fierce and brutal, his booming laughter matching the volume of the thunder around them. Jag dodged and parried, trying to gain a better foothold for a strike or punch, but Bulgaz was relentless and strong. Each swing Jag had to block sent jolts of pressure and sharp pain into his joints, his blade singing from the clash of metal.

Jag's attention was split between the axe-wielding foe before him and the boiling threat spilling danger near Ethan. Humans were so small and fragile; even the smallest thing could harm him.

"Ethan! Get inside!" Jag yelled over his shoulder. "Stay away from the tear!"

"I'll fix this!" Ethan's voice pitched over the noise. "I'll fix this!"

"Is that your little human?" Bulgaz cracked a grin. "Ethan, was it?"

Jag bore his teeth and swung out of anger, earning himself a blow to the ribs and a near miss from Bulgaz's axe. The sting of the blade slicing into the flesh of Jag's chest was a painful token of his error, and his armor ripped as blood stained the fabric.

Bulgaz laughed. "I'll make sure to kill him first. His pretty skin will be stretched out and used as a canvas to keep me cool."

"You go near him, and I'll take your head, Bulgaz." Jag flexed his fingers around his hilt.

A break in the tear made a horrible sound as a screaming chaos boar ripped loose. Its black hooves tore at the ground, mouth wide as it squealed and screamed. Curling tusks splintering at the ends lined its snout. The line of wide, black eyes running the length of its broad skull rolled in a panic at the new surroundings. Fueled by the need to cause mayhem and destruction, the beast raised the sharp spines across its shoulder blades and started to charge.

The chaos boar tore through the backyard, aiming its wild attention towards the screaming humans scrambling to get into the house. Ethan grabbed his friends and started shoving them inside, rushing out to help someone who had fallen. The boar's mouth foamed, and its eyes locked on them, changing course to destroy the weakest of the pack.

Jag swung his blade as hard as he could, the blade soaring

through the small yard and impaling the raging boar to the corn-hole board that cracked under the weight of the animal. It thrashed and tried to struggle free, but the blade had done its job.

Bulgaz's axe blade wedged itself into Jag's left shoulder, splitting flesh and cracking bone.

The pain was white-hot and consuming, the demonic axe burning Jag's blood and sliding against bone as Jag stumbled forward. Jag roared in pain, his body jerking backwards as Bulgaz ripped the blade free and lifted to strike again.

"You damn fool," Bulgaz mocked. "I thought you'd be a challenge. Instead, you throw your weapon to save some worms? Pathetic."

A bright pink trick-or-treat bucket bounced off Bulgaz's horns, and he blinked towards where it was thrown from.

Ethan stood in the yard, forest-green eyes wide, his body still pitched forward from throwing.

"You." Bulgaz snarled.

"Shit." Ethan gulped.

The impact of Bulgaz's body against Jag's shoulder was brutal as Jag tackled the demon to the ground. Pain seared through Jag's wound as he struggled to wrench Bulgaz's axe from his grip, his muscles straining as warm blood poured down his back. The ground shifted around them as they grappled, grass and dirt pressing into cuts, fists pounding into any soft spot Bulgaz could find. Jag could feel his body growing tired, the blood loss and pain causing his strength to wane. His arms shook from fatigue, his head pounded, and Bulgaz's rancid breath made his eyes water.

Jagmarith had never known defeat.

He was Champion of the Blood Wars. Skulls of his fallen enemies were piled high outside of his keep, a testament to his might and brutality. Months ago, a battle such as this would have been thrilling and exciting, a chance to earn another skull for his mountain or die a warrior's death.

Bulgaz pressed the handle of his axe into Jag's throat, leaning down with all his strength to crush his windpipe. The pressure made him choke, and Jag fought back to keep the handle from ending his life.

It would be an honorable death, to lose at the hands of a great demon warrior. He would be stripped of his armor, probably his skin, head, and horns. His body a trophy of a battle well fought.

It was the death Jag had always hoped for, instead of rotting away as an old warrior, alone and useless.

Ethan's voice floated through the haze, the desperation in his voice painful glass shards in his heart.

No.

Jagmarith would not die today.

Ethan needed him.

Jag hooked his horns with Bulgaz's, twisting him off balance and snapping one free.

The other demon screamed at the loss of his horn, his grip giving way and his weapon falling to the ground. Jag sucked in air as the axe fell away and grabbed the severed horn that was still locked with his. Twisting it free, Jag stabbed the horn into Bulgaz's eye, ending the man's wailing and his struggle. The massive body slumped over, and Jag pushed himself free, bloody, achy, but alive.

"Jag!" Ethan tried to rush to his side, but Jag held up a hand for him to wait.

"No time, Ethan. You have to continue your research to close the tear." Jag pushed himself to his feet, hissing from the pain in his shoulder. "There's more coming. Many, many more coming." Jag swallowed the shame in his next words. "I am not going to be able to defeat an army. My people are coming."

Ethan's chest heaved from terror and concern, his eyes jerking to the tear that continued to bulge and stretch.

"Ethan." Jag caught his attention again. "Hurry. Please."

A quiver in Ethan's chin was almost lost as he nodded,

sprinting back up the patio to his laptop. Olivia had his note-book, crowded around the screen with him as they tried desper-ately to find an answer. The guests of the party were inside, peering outside the window and glass doors to the bloody mayhem that had become Olivia's Halloween party.

Three dead demons littered the grass. A chaos boar was pierced to the side of their game board.

And the large tears of reality were about to birth more nightmares.

Jag felt so very, very tired.

The axe was heavy in his hand as he hefted it up, swinging it down with a loud yell to snap Bulgaz's head free from his shoul-ders. It was custom to present a trophy from a battle well fought and won, and while Bulgaz was a pointless shit that had threat-ened Ethan, he was a good fight. Jag groaned in pain as he grabbed the severed head by its only remaining horn, moving towards the tear.

Whatever was pushing on the other side seemed big, stretching high above Jag's form as he glared at the writhing portal. Spite, anger, and exhaustion made Jag throw the disem-bodied skull of Bulgaz at the tear, and he didn't care how petty it made him seem.

The head whipped through the tear without resistance, knocking whatever it was pushing against it back enough to make Jag laugh.

"You think you can kill me with three weak warriors from lesser clans?!" Jag raged, leaning forward to spit into the void. "I am Jagmarith of Clan Montgomery! I will take you with me into the abyss and present your skulls to Satan himself!"

The tear jerked and contracted, causing Jag to pause. For a moment, it almost seemed as if it shrank the smallest bit. Jag understood he was tired and had lost plenty of blood, but he had suffered worse before and never hallucinated. After a moment of hesitation, Jag leaned in and spit again, and the tear jerked and squeezed.

Jag moved in closer, eying the borders of the tear as they slowly began to knit back together, the straining border tightening up but not fully solidifying.

"Sami!" Jag didn't take his eyes off the rift as he felt Sami land on his feet beside him. "What's happening? Do you see it shrinking?"

"Yes, Master. I see it."

"Has Ethan found a solution?" Jag watched the outline of a snapping jaw press against the border, hands pressing beside it as it tried to bite its way through.

"No, Master."

Jag glanced his way before putting his attention back on the threat. "Then why is it shrinking? What's changed?"

Sami's claws made little clicking noises as he wrung his fingers together, the sound a familiar occurrence from the small familiar. "Remember what I said about why the tears are happening, Master?"

"You said they were happening because we did the circle incorrectly."

"Yes, that is why. But what's physically causing the tears is because the tether keeping you here is ripping holes between the realms. Remember?"

Jag jerked his attention back to Sami, whose ears were down flat. "And?"

"And the only way to fix it is for you to go home."

"You said we could fix it by redoing the ceremony!" Jag snapped. "It made it worse!"

"The Retaking overpowered the ceremony, Master." Sami shook his head, big eyes wide with sorrow. "It wasn't Ethan's fault."

"I know it's not Ethan's fault!" Jag roared, and Sami shrank back. The form pressing against the tear began to peel back the barrier, teeth snapping with a long tongue lashing. A hissing scream escaped it as it pushed free, and Jag grabbed it by the skull and pushed it backwards with all of his strength. The moment his hand passed through the tear to shove the creature back, the tear shrank down before flaring back again as he retracted his arm.

Jag stared in horror, the realization setting in like cold stones in his gut.

"The only way to fix it…"

"I'm so sorry, Master," Sami whispered. "We tried."

Jag felt heavy.

Sore.

Bloody.

And so very tired.

The long breath he took to steady himself hurt, and the coldness around his heart threatened to stop it from beating.

"We did," Jag whispered. "We tried so hard."

"You have time," Sami said softly, his clawed hand patting Jag's. "To say goodbye. You should say goodbye."

"Satan." Jag dropped Bulgaz's axe. "I've never felt so small."

"I'll cover you, Master." Sami gripped the axe and dragged it closer, the size of the weapon bigger than him. "Go ahead."

Each footstep felt like Jag was stepping into his own grave, cold and hollow, swallowing him into endless darkness. They had tried so hard. Ethan had tried so hard.

And Jag couldn't fix it. He couldn't make it go away.

And he couldn't stay.

Ethan was still poring over his computer, huddled with Olivia as they went over the text. His brows were drawn down in concentration; various chalk outlines were drawn out on the wooden patio floor. Olivia's boot was splattered with firehornet guts, and Ethan had some beetle juice on his tunic.

"Ethan." Jag stepped up the patio, and Ethan jerked his head up.

"God, Jag. You're bleeding! Let me help you. Sit down. I'll grab something to stop the bleeding."

"Ethan, listen to me." Jag caught Ethan by the shoulders.

"You can talk to me while I help you get patched up," Ethan insisted. "Olivia and I haven't found anything yet, but we're close. We *have* to be close. There's something in here that'll close this, I know it."

"No, there isn't."

"There is. Sit, Jag. You need to rest. Olivia, can you—" Ethan trailed off as Jag pulled him into a hug, holding him tight. Jag felt Ethan's arms wrap around him and squeeze, his forest eyes watching him as Jag pulled back.

"I cannot keep you safe from my clans, Ethan. If more come through that tear, I will fall. You will die, and I cannot let that happen."

"It won't," Ethan insisted, sounding more confident and firm than he ever had. "We will find a solution, Jag. I swear we will."

"There is a solution. If I pass through the tear, it will seal. The tether won't cause any more rips, and you'll be safe."

Ethan's brows knitted, his head shaking in disapproval. "What does that mean? What are you saying?"

Jag felt his heart tearing, pieces crumbling into ashes inside of his chest.

"I have to go, Ethan. It's the only way."

The hope in Ethan's eyes melted, revealing the panic and hurt resting just below the surface.

"No."

"I'm sorry, Ethan."

"No!" Ethan grabbed Jag's hand, squeezing tight. "No way in hell I'm letting you leave." He jabbed at his laptop. "There's a solution in there. I'll find it."

Behind them, the tear pulsed and ripped higher up the sky, and Jag could make out the piercing tips of blades trying to cut through the barrier. Sami gripped the axe handle, ready to attempt a swing they both knew he couldn't do.

"I just need more time. Just a little more time—" Ethan pleaded, his confidence leaking from his voice. "I will fix this! I have to fix this!"

"This is bigger than you, Ethan. You cannot fix it."

"I can!" Ethan's voice snapped, faltering as tears broke loose. "I can make it right. I have to. I *have* to, Jag!"

It tore at Jag's soul to feel Ethan jerk away from his grip, trying desperately to get back to work. Olivia had stepped back, mouth covered, tears falling silently. Ethan's breath was stuttered with hiccups as he tried to tear through his notebook, screaming in frustration as Jag pulled him away by the shoulders.

"Ethan..."

"Master!" Sami warned from the yard. "I can hear the battle horn!"

Jag gathered his breath and swallowed, not allowing himself to feel the sting of tears.

"You told me the only way you'd leave my side is if I sent you away," Ethan snapped, his voice watery and hurt. "I didn't send you away. You can't leave me, Jag."

"I have to break that vow. I'm sorry." Jag cupped his cheek. "Never in my life have I felt something so powerful and wonderful as loving you, Ethan of Clan Montgomery. Until my dying breath, I will hold you in my memories."

Ethan's face twisted in pain, sobs racking his form. "I'm so sorry, Jag. I'm so sorry."

"Never apologize to me," Jag whispered, kissing his forehead. "Be brave, my love. My scholar. My Ethan."

"I love you," Ethan managed through his tears, his voice a husk of pain and misery. "I love you so much."

"Master!" Sami yelled in alarm. "Hurry! We have to go now!"

Jag shut his eyes a moment, breathing in the last bit of Ethan he could. His hair smelled like citrus. Sugar on his breath. Salt on his cheeks. His fingers gripped Jag's wrists like they were his lifeline.

I love you.

Jag let his tears fall as he turned away from Ethan, unable to look back.

The tear was steadily climbing, the wide gaping barrier stretched thin with an army pressing down. Teeth gnashed, and clawed hands ripped and began to puncture through, the steady blare of war horns drifting across realms.

The Retaking was a breath away from breaching. Jag began to run, grabbing his sword from the dead chaos boar and roaring his own battle cry.

He'd fight them all.

He'd kill those who threatened this world.

They would pay for stealing him away from Ethan, and they would know that Jagmarith, Green Ranger of Clan Montgomery, stole The Retaking from the demons.

They would remember his name.

15

CLAN MONTGOMERY

Everything hurt.

Breathing hurt.

Standing hurt.

Living hurt.

Ethan felt like his heart had folded in on itself and shattered so completely that he'd never feel whole again.

He had failed so utterly at everything. His research failed him; his ability to fix the portal had failed.

He had failed.

Jag's words replayed over in his head, bittersweet and painful, crushing him until Ethan couldn't stand anymore. Jag had loved him, fought for him, and was surely going to die for him. And there was nothing Ethan could do.

Tears blurred his vision, warping the surrounding nightmare in messy blobs of color. The sky churned high above, the smell of blood and acid choked him as he tried to breathe. A distant sound of a bellowing horn was leaking through the tear, and Ethan knew he should be afraid.

But he was so numb to it all. Somewhere beside him, Olivia was trying to pull him inside, but he didn't want to move.

He had to see it through to the end. Some masochistic part of his soul had to see Jag leave, to see the tear heal and his life crumble. A selfish part of him hoped it wouldn't work, that Jag would be stuck on earth with him, so they could at least be together.

But that wasn't fair. It was a horrible wish. Ethan hated himself for it.

Jag's bellowing cry tore through the yard, charging the chasm of demonic magic that pulsed with hellish creatures trying to rip free. He was beautiful, even bloody and exhausted. Black blood stained the ripped Halloween costume, his long hair sticking to his neck, dried blood across his bruised face.

Jag, the demon who had stumbled into his life nine months ago, who baked headless gingerbread men and collected skulls for Ethan, raised his sword and dove headfirst towards the barrier between earth and hell.

For Ethan.

His Ethan.

My love.

Ethan shut his eyes tight and turned away, feeling sick and dizzy from anguish.

The tear snapped shut, zipping up with a crack of thunder that melted the sky back to its normal color. Hesitantly, Ethan blinked up at the sky, feeling the storm fade. The green and black clouds dissipated, the wind calmed, and the large wounds in reality were gone.

Ethan knew he should have felt relieved, but he didn't.

It hurt.

It hurt so goddamn much.

Someone was shaking his arm, but he barely registered it. His notebook of research notes slid off his lap and to the ground. What a piece of shit that turned out to be. So much wasted time.

He should have just spent more time with Jag instead of poring over his useless research.

"Ethan!" Olivia's voice pierced through as she shook his shoulders. "Ethan, look!"

"Yeah, I know." He rubbed his tired eyes. "I know. I see the sky."

"No, you jackass! Look!" Olivia grabbed him by the head and turned his eyes towards the yard.

Everything froze.

Ethan's heart stopped beating. His breath jerked to a halt.

Standing in the yard, looking bloody, tired, exhausted, and deeply confused, was a dream come true.

Jag.

Ethan's body was moving before he could register if he had truly lost his mind. He vaulted over a body, tripped over a broken Halloween decoration, and recovered just in time to slam into Jag. He felt real. He smelled real. His pained grunt sounded very real.

Ethan wrapped his arms around him and squeezed, refusing to let go.

"How?" Ethan whispered, his face pressed into Jag's shoulder. "How is this real? Did I die? Are we dead?"

"I would hope death is less painful." Jag's hand smoothed over his curls and down his back. "But I am very unsure what's going on."

Ethan lifted his chin to look at him. "How are you still here? I saw you run into the tear."

Jag shook his head, glancing around the yard. "I do not know."

A fissure in the air warped the surroundings, a much gentler version of the tear formed with an oval shape. Instead of jerking and pulsating, it stood static and calm, like a standing pool of rippling water.

"What the hell is that?" Ethan eyed the doorway warily, too exhausted to even be afraid of it.

"I...do not know." Jag tightened his grip on his sword, ready for what might step through.

"Master!" Sami came over, dragging the heavy axe behind him through the grass.

"Sami, what's going on?" Jag nodded at the oval portal. "What is this? What happened to the tears?"

"The Oath was completed!" Sami grinned with his needle teeth, ears perked up in joy. "With the completion of the Oath, the magic is no longer unstable because there is a clear pathway back home."

"The...Oath." Jag blinked in confusion.

"Yes!" Sami hooked his arm around the handle of the axe to keep it from dropping to the ground, but freed up his hands to explain. "The Oath has strict rules that are bound by magic. The longer the Oath went without being fulfilled, the more unstable the tether became. Now that it's complete, the other demons cannot breach through and attack!"

"Wait." Ethan shook his head, his foggy thoughts slowly clearing. "How did we complete the Oath?"

Sami tapped his chin with his clawed fingers. "If I remember correctly, weren't you trying to make someone jealous?"

Ethan and Jag slowly turned to face the patio, staring down the Halloween guests that were gathered by the door watching them.

David stared at them, his cheeks slowly flushing red as Ivan gaped at him.

"You're *jealous* of him?" Ivan balked, offended to his very well-toned core.

"No!"

Ivan presented Ethan, Jag, and Sami to him like David couldn't see them standing there. "The demon, his goblin, and your ex say otherwise, *honey.*"

"I'm a familiar," Sami mumbled.

"Well...he...it was romantic!" David pleaded. "Jag called him his clan and rushed off to die for him. C'mon!"

"Oh. Well. Excuse the shit out of me. I do stuff for you."

"When we saw that cockroach in the kitchen, you locked me out of the bedroom yelling 'every man for himself' and left me to die!" David flailed his arms. "It was flying, and I was terrified!"

"Cockroaches and demons are different, asshole!" Ivan stomped his foot and pushed through the guests, forcing his way back into the house with David on his heels.

Ethan couldn't help but huff a tired laugh. "I cannot believe after all this, that's what saved us." Jag's fingers tightening on the base of his neck caught his attention. The sad, weak smile on Jag's lips left a cold feeling in his gut.

"The tears may be gone, but that doesn't mean I can stay, Ethan."

"What? Why? We're safe! It's—it's done!"

"It stabilized the tether *for now*." Jag shook his head. "But if I stay, this will happen again. Especially now that the Oath is done."

"He's right, Ethan," Sami chimed in, sounding guilty. "We'll be right back at the apocalypse again in a couple months."

Ethan's stomach twisted, and he felt the blood drain from his head.

His mind began to race, bouncing from one solution to the next. Ethan would go with Jag.

To hell? Likely not.

They could prolong his stay by limiting their touching.

Like Jag would go for that. And it's still finite.

Maybe they could keep the portal open somehow? A spell or another—

"Oath! Another Oath!" Ethan blurted in excitement.

"What?" Jag blinked, and Sami cocked his head, ears leveling in confusion.

"We need another Oath. No—something better." Ethan ran back to the patio, scooping up his notebook and began flipping through the pages like a frantic madman. The scribbles all seemed to run together, but he was searching for a very particular passage.

"Ethan..." Jag began, sounding uncertain.

"This!" Ethan grinned, bringing the notebook over and tapping the page. "We can do this one."

Jag peered over the page. "Vow of the Heart?"

Sami gasped, his ears flying up. "Oooooh!"

"What is that?" Jag looked to his familiar, who was grinning so big, Ethan was worried his face would get stuck that way.

"Better than an Oath! Much better! This one isn't conditional. It's a pact." Sami laced his fingers together. "A vow to one another, binding your souls together in unholy matrimony."

Jag stared at his familiar for a long moment before turning his churning, molten gaze to Ethan.

"...You want to marry me."

"Yeah," Ethan breathed out with a laugh. "Sorry, I didn't get you a ring."

"A ring of what?"

"It's not as simple as just a marriage," Sami added, his ears lowering but not losing their excitement. "I believe for humans, it's more of a contract. That contact has rules and expectations and can be broken." He mimicked snapping something in half with his hands. "This vow binds your souls together. Your lives would be intertwined, until death. And it cannot be undone once it is set in place."

A wave of unease washed over Ethan. "Does that mean...I would have a demon's lifespan? Live for hundreds of years?"

"No." Sami's ears went flat. "Jag would have a human lifespan. Master, you will die in only a small collection of years if Ethan lives out a natural human lifespan."

"If we do this vow, you can stay here with me," Ethan explained. "We could have a life here together. You'd have to be human most of the time, but I promise you I'll do whatever it takes to make you happy, Jag. I promise." Ethan chewed his bottom lip and squeezed Jag's fingers. "But if you want to go home, I won't stop you, and I won't beg you to stay. I'm asking you to give up a huge portion of your lifespan, and I understand the weight of that. You've done more for me than I could ever repay. I want you to be happy."

Jag's throat bobbed as he swallowed. "I cannot fathom a life without you, Ethan. Short or long. If you'll have me, I will stay by your side."

Jag's lips had never tasted so good. Ethan took his handsome demon by the face and kissed him, smiling as Jag lifted him up off the ground to deepen the passionate embrace.

Olivia made a gasping, sobby squeak of joy as she clapped, some of her party guests joining in the celebration.

David and Ivan were long gone, which was good. They weren't invited to the wedding.

The Vow was much less involved than the Oath.

Since the Oath had parameters of revenge and diabolical undertones, it needed much more magic and ceremony to complete. The Vow, on the other hand, was simple. The words spoken were constructed to tie the threads of their love and connection together, binding their life essence into a harmonious, beautiful knot.

Ethan read the entire vow and was amazed to hear Jag repeat it back—actually pronouncing it correctly. Jag's multiple tongues produced dual and triple sounds at the same time, the language stunning as much as it was haunting.

"I think…" Ethan flipped through the pages of his notebook. "I think that's all of it. Did it work?"

"I don't feel any different." Jag felt his chest. "Do you?"

"No. I don't know if we're supposed to, and the door is still open in the yard." Ethan exhaled and checked his notebook again. "Okay, I missed something—"

"Maybe don't try again yet." Olivia placed her hand over the pages. "Last time we tried that, literally all hell broke loose."

"Ah. Fair." Ethan felt heat flush his cheeks. She had a point, even if it did sting. The oval door in the yard rippled like someone had touched the surface, and Jag grabbed his sword.

"Fuck, what now?" Olivia grabbed a broken table leg, and Ethan held his breath. A tall, thin creature emerged from the door, antlers first. It stood a good seven feet, excluding the midnight-black antlers that rose up in sharp spikes. The face was a mixture of a deer's long skull and a human's, with flat teeth and a wild death grin. Rags hung from its boney form, covered in bells and charms that chimed softly as it began to float their way.

"Oh, thank Satan." Jag breathed out in relief. "It's just a messenger."

"A what?" Ethan hid behind him. "Is it friendly? It looks terrifying!"

"They are benign creatures who deliver messages. They will not harm you."

"Oh." Ethan followed Jag down the steps, holding up his hand in the greeting Jag had taught him months ago. "In that case...um. Greetings, messenger."

The creature tilted its head and said nothing.

"You just greeted him as a distant aunt on your father's side," Sami whispered, and Ethan dropped his hand quickly.

Jag cleared his throat. "Sorry, That Which Sees. He's a good man, but he is bad with greetings."

The messenger straightened his head and presented folded pieces of parchment in his long fingers that resembled spindly spider legs. Jag took them with a nod, unfolding one paper and then the other.

"What is it?" Ethan peeked around Jag's shoulder to see. The language was similar to that of the book, but Ethan could tell the symbols were a bit more stylized and bold.

Jag was silent a long time. "It's a permit."

"A what?"

"A permit. A permanent permit to stay here." Jag showed him like Ethan would know what it said. "This is so no one from home can use my existence here to start a war with the humans. It allows me to be here legally and not cause rifts."

Ethan blinked at the paper, then up at Jag. "It worked?"

Jag's grin was crooked, his teeth a little sharp in his demon form. "It worked."

"Holy shit! It worked!" Ethan ducked under Jag's arm to hug him. "What's the other paper?"

"Documentation of our clans merging." Jag pointed out the lettering on the paper, which was signed and stamped with a blood-colored wax. "Clan Bonereaver and Clan Montgomery are now one."

"Wow." Had Jag's arm not been around him, Ethan was sure he would have floated away. "That's so amazing. I didn't expect to get a marriage license from this." He examined the signature and stamp, the embossed crest pressed into the wax a twisted horned goat with symbols around it. "Who signed this?"

Jag lifted his brows. "Satan, of course."

"...Beg pardon?"

"We must tip the messenger so it can return. Otherwise, it will steal one of our eyes as payment."

Ethan felt himself pale. "I thought you said they were harmless?"

"If you tip." Jag glanced around before plucking a neon green, plastic spider ring from a dropped cupcake. He presented it to the bony creature, who plucked it from his palm with those long, spider-leg fingers. After a quick inspection, it was placed among its charms, its mouth falling open silently.

"Is...is that my strawberry magnet?" Ethan studied it as the messenger turned and made its way back to the portal, slipping through as quickly as it had come.

The door vanished.

"Ethan." Jag smiled down at his new mate, or husband, or whatever demons called their significant others. "I am very happy to be one with you, and I want to please you for the rest of our lives. But my shoulder is in great pain, and I'm very tired."

"Me too." Ethan rubbed his back, smiling up at him. "Let's go home, Green Ranger."

EPILOGUE

Jagmarith, second son of Bolor'gath, Champion of the Retaking, wearer of the Green Ranger armor of Clan Montgomery, was hard at work on a batch of his famous gingerbread demons.

It had taken many batches of trial and error to get the dough just right, and finding a mold with horns and tails had been tricky. The demon cookies always had a battlefield of slaughtered victims iced with jelly and gumdrops, mostly cinnamon flavor to add a little kick. The human ones were a bit more traditional and didn't have nearly as many casualties on the battlefield.

It was a fair compromise.

"Looks good." Ethan stole a bit of icing as Jag concentrated on outlining the fondant guts. "Which battle is this?"

"Mangle Tide," Jag answered absently, fixing some jellybean armor. "I took many spines that day. I made them out of licorice."

"I can see that." Ethan's playful smirk meant he was hiding something. Jag set his candy aside and lifted a brow.

"What are you hiding, Ethan?"

"Me? What?" Ethan scoffed. "I'm not hiding anything."

"You are a bad liar."

Ethan hummed and wiggled his brows. "What could it be?"

"Did you hear back about the job?" Jag tried, and Ethan shrugged a shoulder up.

"I may have heard through the grapevine that I should be expecting a call about a position starting in the spring." Ethan bit his lip in a teasing grin. "But that's not it."

"Did you plan another vacation to the beach so I can take my revenge against the seagulls?"

"Nope." Ethan hooked his arm around Jag's. "How about I show you?"

"I still wish to get my revenge, Ethan." Jag followed as Ethan pulled him out of the kitchen. "They stole from me and insulted me with their cries and by shitting in my ice cream."

"I know. You'll get your chance." Ethan pulled him into the living room, where a large object was covered in a festive sheet.

"What is this?" Jag cocked his head as Ethan stepped over to the object. "It's massive."

"It's your first ever Christmas/anniversary present!" Ethan beamed. "A year ago today, I summoned you to make my ex jealous by going to a stupid party. Since then, we've been through hell and back, and I wanted to get you something extra special."

"Ethan. You didn't need to get me any type of treasure. You have nothing to prove with me."

"I know. I wanted to." He grinned wide as he tugged the sheet free. "Taa-daa!"

Under the sheet was the giant, gaping maw of a large beast Jag had never seen before. The animal had a massive snout lined with dagger teeth, a giant nasal cavity, and powerful jaws.

"What is this?" Jag examined the creature in awe, feeling the black bone.

"Okay, so it's not real bone, but it's a cast. The real one is in a museum we can visit. But!" Ethan gave the skull a proud pat. "This is the largest, most badass predator that ever roamed the earth. It could crush the bones of animals ten times its size and was the ruling apex predator of its time. The only thing that could wipe it from existence was a massive meteor that crashed into the planet and wiped out almost all life."

Jag traced his fingers over the teeth, giving his mate a skeptical glance. "Is this like how I found out dragons aren't real? Is this a fairy tale?"

"It's real! I promise. Dinosaurs were absolutely real, and this is the king of them all. The tyrant lizard." Ethan's face winced. "Does it still count if it's a cast? Is it still a trophy?"

Since Jag had never heard of making a cast for a skull, he wasn't sure how it fit in demon society. But he no longer abided by the ways of his people. If it was from Ethan, it was trophy enough for him.

"Yes." Jag gave the snout a pat. "It counts. This is a good trophy, Ethan. Thank you."

Ethan's wide smile made Jag feel warm inside. Forest-green eyes sparkled as Jag gave him a kiss.

"Merry Christmas, Ethan," Jag mumbled against Ethan's lips.

"Mm. Merry Christmas, Jag."

The End

ABOUT THE AUTHOR

Maz Maddox has always wanted to be an author.

Well, almost always.

At first she wanted to be a dinosaur, but that turned out to be extremely difficult. Giving up on her dreams to be a towering Allosaurus, she discovered her love for amazing stories and started writing her own.

Maybe one day she'll try the dinosaur thing again.

Follow Maz:

www.mazmaddox.com
Newsletter signup: www.subscribepage.com/subtomaz
mazmaddox@gmail.com

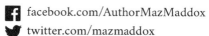 facebook.com/AuthorMazMaddox
twitter.com/mazmaddox
 instagram.com/mazmaddox

ALSO BY MAZ MADDOX

Stallion Ridge series

Heartache & Hoofbeats

Claw Marks & Card Games

Suspects & Scales

Rocks & Railways

Mimics & Mayhem

Runes, Ruin & Redemption

Fate & Fortune

RELIC series

Smash & Grab

Sink or Swim

King & Queen

CPSIA information can be obtained
at www.ICGtesting.com
Printed in the USA
LVHW100106010622
720160LV00007B/255